LINDA WILLIAMS JACKSON

A Sky Full of Stars

HOUGHTON MIFFLIN HARCOURT
BOSTON NEW YORK

ALSO BY LINDA WILLIAMS JACKSON

Midnight Without a Moon

Copyright © 2018 by Linda Williams Jackson

All rights reserved. For information about permission to reproduce selections from this book, write to Permissions, Houghton Mifflin Harcourt Publishing Company, 3 Park Avenue, 19th Floor, New York, New York 10016.

www.hmhco.com

The text was set in Fairfield.
Art by Sarah J. Coleman
Book design by Sharismar Rodriguez

The Library of Congress Cataloging-in-Publication data is on file.
ISBN 978-0-544-80065-6

Manufactured in the United States of America
DOC 10 9 8 7 6 5 4 3 2 1
4500688768

This book is dedicated to my first critique partners—

Shelley Sly

and

Peaches D. Ledwidge.

Thank you for being there when I needed you most.

STILLWATER, MISSISSIPPI

1955

November

Chapter One

MONDAY, NOVEMBER 7

My grandpa, papa, used to say that gratitude was the key to happiness. If that was true, then I would never be happy.

With the chill of November upon us, and all of Mr. Robinson's cotton picked clean off every stalk in his fields, I was finally able to attend school like my younger brother, Fred Lee, and my older cousin Queen. But instead of school, where I should have been that beautiful fall day, I was cooped up in Mrs. Robinson's kitchen, contemplating whether I should clean up the mess left behind by her cackling church club or pretend I had gone mad and add to it. Knowing the latter was impossible to actually get away with without my grandma, Ma Pearl, slapping me into the middle of the next week, one after the other, I held Mrs. Robinson's fancy gold-rimmed plates over the empty bucket she had given me and scraped off leftovers. At least our hogs could be grateful for the slop.

Down the hall, happy hums flowed from a content Ma Pearl as she dusted every item in Mrs. Robinson's already spotless bedroom. Of course she was happy. While Papa was on his return trip from Blytheville, Arkansas, where he'd attended his brother Charlie's funeral, she had seized the opportunity to keep me out of school for the day. Had it been left to her, I would be kept out of school not just one day but every day. "A seventh grade education is more'n enough," she'd said back in August when she tried to make me quit school for good.

So this morning when she yelled, "Git up, gal. Git dressed. You helpin' me this moan'n," I knew she didn't mean baking biscuits or frying eggs. I had heard her the night before complaining about how she "sho' didn't wanna hafta clean up after Miz Robinson and that nasty bunch a womens tomorrow." So there I was in her place, cleaning up after Mrs. Robinson and that "nasty bunch a womens" who were supposedly having Bible study.

Laughter exploded in the parlor. Didn't these ladies have anything better to do on a Monday afternoon than giggle? There I was scraping practically full meals off plates, throwing good food to hogs, and they had nothing better to do at one in the afternoon than laugh—well, Bible study, supposedly, from ten till noon, then chitchat over coconut cake and coffee for the rest of the day. And their husbands still came home to a clean house and a full meal.

Like my good friend Hallelujah Jenkins always said, if

they'd spend a little more time with the good Lord on Sunday like colored folks did, then they wouldn't have to make up for it on Monday.

I stomped into the dining room and grabbed another stack of plates. On one of them lay a barely eaten ham and cheese sandwich. By my estimate, two bites had been taken. I peered out of the dining room toward the hallway for any sign of Ma Pearl. Chatter flowed cheerfully from the parlor —so no need to worry about the Cackling Church Club. I placed the stack of plates back on the table and snatched the sandwich off the top one.

My teeth sank into it. Lord, it was good. The ham was nothing like what our poor slaughtered hogs supplied us. It was tender, easy to chew, and beyond delicious. And the cheese? A flavor I'd never experienced—slightly smoky, almost heavenly.

I took another bite of the sandwich, closed my eyes, and savored every chew. I knew I should have stopped after two bites, but the sandwich begged me to finish. I didn't realize how hungry I was until I'd taken the last bite. I hadn't eaten since six o'clock, and then only biscuits. Fred Lee and Queen had eaten all the eggs before I got a chance to even get to the kitchen. And for that I fault Ma Pearl, seeing I had to take extra care in dressing myself to ensure I was halfway decent enough to cross the Robinson threshold.

Another partially eaten sandwich taunted me from a plate. I resisted by stacking other plates on top of it. But my growling stomach betrayed me, forcing me to put the plates back down and grab the half-eaten sandwich. My mouth opened wide, and my teeth sank deep. I couldn't stop myself from moaning, because this one, too, was undeniably delicious.

"Rose Lee Carter!" came a whispered shout.

I froze.

I didn't bother turning all the way around. From the corner of my eye, I spotted Ma Pearl's massive frame blocking the doorway to the dining room. My heart raced faster than a scared rabbit's. How could I have been foolish enough to let Ma Pearl sneak up on me?

"Gal, what the devil is you doin'?"

I couldn't answer because my mouth was full. Nor could I swallow, because a lump filled my throat. So there I stood, my mouth stuffed with sandwich, my body stiff with shame, as I waited for my grandma to storm into Mrs. Robinson's dining room and knock me to kingdom come.

When I didn't answer her, Ma Pearl charged into the room like a raging bull. She stopped inches from my face. With her nostrils flaring, she swept the remainder of the sandwich from my hand. It landed on the gleaming wood floor.

I shut my eyes and braced myself for a slap.

But instead of a slap, I got a plate shoved into my hands.

One by one, Ma Pearl snatched them off the table. When she spoke, she kept her voice low but firm. "I didn't brang you over here to ack like no dirn fool." She began piling the dishes in my arms. "If that woman wanted you to eat these leftover sammiches, she'da gave you a bag."

She paused and frowned at me. "Did she give you a bag?"

I managed to force the lump of ham, cheese, and bread down my throat. "No, ma'am," I muttered.

"What she give you?"

"A bucket," I said quietly, my eyes darting from the floor to Ma Pearl's gaze, then back to the floor again.

"So why is you eatin' this food?"

Because it's perfectly good food that these ungrateful women just played over because they don't know what it's like to be hungry.

Ma Pearl gestured toward the table. "This food meant for the hogs, not for the humans."

The hogs ain't the only somethin' hungry on this place. Hogs shouldn't eat ham anyway. They are *ham!*

When I still said nothing, Ma Pearl's giant hand whapped me on the shoulder. I stumbled sideways.

"Quit ack'n like a triflin' nigga," she said. "I feed you at home."

My shoulder throbbed with pain, but I didn't dare raise

my hand to rub it. Besides, I needed both hands to ensure I didn't drop Mrs. Robinson's precious plates. Anticipating another powerful lick from Ma Pearl's heavy hand, my body grew stiffer, scared to breathe. But instead of smacking me again, she turned on her heels and stormed from the dining room. Her huffing seemed to ring in my ears until she reached Mrs. Robinson's bedroom at the end of the hall.

Happy it didn't get knocked to the floor, my body relaxed a bit, but shame burned in it like an August sun. Knowing I had no choice, I swallowed that shame and carried the armful of plates to the kitchen. After all the plates and saucers had been scraped clean, I returned to the dining room to collect the lipstick-stained, half-full cups of coffee and tea. Near one of the cups lay a beige, lace-trimmed handkerchief. The swirly blue letters *KJM* told me it belonged to Mrs. Jamison —Kay Marie Jamison—who was known around Stillwater for having her initials monogrammed on almost everything she owned, with the *J* always prominent and large. I suppose that was a privilege of having a husband who owned a clothing store.

I stood there for a moment and debated whether to leave the handkerchief on the table or take it to the parlor. Since Mrs. Jamison was known for having a persistent runny nose, she probably needed that handkerchief. But I reasoned that a rich lady like that should have more than one handkerchief in her purse.

After making a couple of trips from the dining room to the kitchen, I realized how silly it was to leave the handkerchief lying on the table. I snatched it up and headed to the parlor. Outside the parlor entry, I froze. How foolish would I look interrupting Mrs. Robinson and her guests over a handkerchief? I decided to drop it in the hallway and allow Mrs. Jamison to assume *she'd* dropped it.

But what if Mrs. Robinson came out and found the handkerchief lying there? She would probably blame me for not doing a good job of cleaning up. Even though it was a simple one, the decision swirled in me like a storm. I clenched the handkerchief in my fist. I knew what I had to do. I had to interrupt the Cackling Church Club and give Mrs. Jamison her handkerchief.

I took a deep breath, released it slowly, then stepped toward the parlor entry. And the second I did, the word *niggers* slammed my ears so hard that it almost knocked me to the floor.

Chapter Two

MONDAY, NOVEMBER 7

As I stood at the parlor entry, I don't know who appeared more flustered—me or Mrs. Robinson and her friends.

Mrs. Robinson, her face red, stammered when she spoke. "Oh . . . um . . . Rose, did you . . . need something?"

My sweaty palms told me I should have minded my own business and left the handkerchief lying on the dining room table.

I took a hard swallow before I spoke.

My voice failed me anyway. "I-I—um."

Mrs. Robinson pursed her lips.

I took a deep breath and composed myself. I held up the handkerchief and quickly said, "Somebody left this."

With a sigh, Mrs. Robinson rolled her eyes toward the ceiling. A few of the other ladies reacted similarly, as if to say, "How dare this foolish girl interrupt us for something as frivolous as a forgotten handkerchief!"

When I cast my eyes toward the floor, wishing I could melt into it, a throat cleared.

I glanced up and spotted the petite, smartly dressed Mrs. Jamison staring at me. When she beckoned me toward her, fear filled my heart.

Nervously, I walked over to her and placed the handkerchief in her outstretched hand.

She peered directly into my eyes and said gently, "Thank you, child."

I knew I wasn't supposed to, but I couldn't help but stare straight back at her. I'd heard that she was a kind lady, even allowing her colored maid to enter her home through the front door—and not just the kitchen. I'd also heard that she even invited her maid to dine at the table with her occasionally. I didn't know whether either of those things were true, but I did know that as she stared at me, her eyes seemed as comforting as hot coffee on a cold morning.

And her smile was equally comforting.

I smiled back.

I'm not sure what overcame me, but with Mrs. Jamison looking *at me*—and not *through me*—smiling at me that way, I was unable to move. My mind and body were locked in a trance.

But Mrs. Robinson quickly broke it. "Rose!" she snapped.

I glanced around. All the women were staring at me. Some of them with their mouths slightly open.

Mrs. Robinson cleared her throat. She stared steely-eyed

at me and said, "While I'm sure Mrs. Jamison is grateful for your kind gesture, it is very rude of you to stand there gawking at her like that."

I opened my mouth to apologize, but before one word came out, Mrs. Robinson pointed toward the hallway.

Her mouth said nothing, but her face said, *Git!*

My heartbeat quickened as I scurried from the room.

I knew I should have hurried to the kitchen, but my heart was pumping blood to my head so fast that I thought it would explode. I leaned against the wall outside the parlor and placed my hand over my heart to steady it.

I couldn't believe I'd just stood there and stared in the face of a white woman as if she was my grandmother and I was her darling little granddaughter. What if Ma Pearl had been nearby and heard Mrs. Robinson chastise me like that?

I took several deep breaths and said a quick prayer in hopes that Mrs. Robinson wouldn't mention the incident to Ma Pearl. And just as my weakened legs regained enough strength to carry me back to the kitchen, I heard one of the women say with a haughty sniff, "You see, Rebecca, this is just what I'm talking about. Ever since that trial, the coloreds have gotten beside themselves."

My body stiffened. The voice sounded like the same one who'd hissed "niggers" just before I stepped into the parlor. And what did she mean by "gotten beside themselves"? Was she talking about me? I hadn't meant to stare at Mrs. Jamison like that. And I certainly couldn't help that her warm smile invited me to smile back.

There was a reply to the woman's comment, but it was whispered and muffled.

Though I knew I shouldn't have, I pressed my ear to the wall. If these ladies were talking about me, I wanted to know what they were saying—especially if Mrs. Robinson was thinking about reporting my actions to Ma Pearl.

I couldn't quite make out what the woman was saying, but I did pick up on the words "NAACP," "trial," and "shameful." I couldn't believe they were still talking about that trial of Roy Bryant and his brother J. W. Milam, the men who killed Emmett Till.

My friend Hallelujah Jenkins said that it's all anyone in Stillwater—white and colored—had talked about for the last month and a half. White folks thought they had been treated unfairly by the colored press, especially *Jet* magazine, whom they claimed had given Mississippi a bad name with their so-called "one-sided" reporting.

And colored folks certainly felt we had been treated unfairly when a jury announced that those two killers had not murdered Emmett Till, a colored boy who was said to have whistled at a white woman. They were free to go on with their lives, while that poor boy had lost his. And if they could get away with such a gruesome murder even after eyewitnesses testified against them, then there was no telling what could happen to colored people in Mississippi next.

My ears perked up when another voice came through a bit more clearly.

"After all those boys have been through, I can't believe they might make them go back to court."

Boys? What boys? Roy Bryant and J. W. Milam? The only boy involved in that case was Emmett Till. And he was dead, at only fourteen. Just a year older than me.

And what did she mean by go back to court? Who was going back to court? And why?

That storm swirled in my stomach again. I longed to do the right thing—to rush back to the kitchen and take my ears away from eavesdropping on Mrs. Robinson and her friends. I was potentially in enough trouble already if Mrs. Robinson decided to tell Ma Pearl about what happened in the parlor. I knew I should have left, but my legs wouldn't move. I felt like the apostle Paul, who said when he wanted to do right, sometimes, he just couldn't. I pressed my ear against the wall and strained to listen.

The next voice I heard belonged to Mrs. Robinson. "I wish the coloreds up north would realize how happy the coloreds are down here. Then they'd quit runnin' down here trying to change things."

"I know all of ours are happy," someone interjected.

"Ours too," came another. "Matter of fact, Allen and I are thinking about getting indoor plumbing for all our people."

"Oh, how nice!" came a voice that sounded very much like Mrs. Robinson's. But surely it couldn't have been her, seeing that they had been promising to give us indoor plumbing for over two years now. Instead, we still had to use that stinky outdoor toilet and pump our water from a well in the backyard.

"It's too bad those colored newspapers and magazines never report the good things that go on in the South," someone said. "They should come down here and see how nice our colored schools are."

Lively "amens" bounced around the room, until Mrs. Robinson interrupted with "Y'all heard they went ahead and integrated over there in Hoxie, right?"

"Did the governmen—" someone began in a hushed tone.

"Nooo," Mrs. Robinson interrupted. "Their superintendent said it was the right thing to do in the sight of God. They just went ahead and integrated. Nobody told 'em they had to."

"Lord-a-mercys" replaced the "amens."

I didn't know where Hoxie was, but I sure knew that integration was something that white folks seemed to fear more than anything else. I couldn't tell exactly what was happening on the other side of that wall, but I sensed that the mood had changed. Especially when I heard one of the ladies begin to cry.

"Lord, what is this world coming to?" the sobbing woman said. "Arkansas is right next door to us. We could be next."

Sofas creaked and feet shuffled as the women gathered to soothe whoever was sobbing.

"Hoxie is allowing the colored children to attend the white schools because they don't have the funds to build proper colored schools," said Mrs. Robinson. "Our colored schools are very nice, so we don't have to worry about all that integration nonsense."

Very nice, huh? You moved tombstones from the colored graveyard and built a brick school over it. I bet you don't want the colored press to report that!

I wanted so badly to escape to the kitchen before I heard even more that I would regret. Plus, my heart thumped rapidly at the thought of Ma Pearl suddenly sauntering out—or worse, one of the ladies coming out of the parlor—and catching me. But my legs simply wouldn't cooperate. They kept me clinging to that wall.

"I hope you're right" came the sobbing voice. "People are much happier with their own kind."

"What colored child would want to endure the same

instructions as a white child anyway?" asked Mrs. Robinson. "I don't think they'd ever be able to keep up."

"The poor dears," someone said. "I imagine it would be pure torture."

Now the only noise that came from the parlor was mixed chatter. All I could discern from it was "happy," "colored," and "separate."

I'd had enough of eavesdropping on the Cackling Church Club and was ready to head back to the kitchen. But as soon as my foot edged from the wall, I heard a voice that stopped me. It was Mrs. Jamison.

"I think we could all learn a thing or two from the folks over in Hoxie," she said. "The government shouldn't have to force us to integrate our schools. There's no point in throwing good money away building more schools when we have plenty of room for all of Stillwater's children in the white schools."

"Mercy, Kay!" someone gasped. "Have you lost your *mind?*"

The whole house grew still. So still that I swear I could hear the sun shining.

"No, I have not lost my mind," Mrs. Jamison finally said. "What sense is there to keep building all these schools just to keep the children separate?"

The next voice was sharp. "Because that's just the way

things are. And it's the way they should be. If our colored folks wanted their children to go to the same schools as white children, then they'd move up north like the rest of them. The fact that they stay here proves that they're happy here."

"Kay," Mrs. Robinson said gently. "Imagine if this was when your boys were younger. I don't think you'd feel the same way if your children were still in school."

The "amens" returned.

"I've always felt this way," Mrs. Jamison retorted.

The sharp voice responded. "Is that why you sent Jason to Yale and let him marry a dumb Yankee?"

"Now, now, Charlotte," said Mrs. Robinson. "Let's not get carried away. This is a Bible study after all."

I cringed. I didn't see even one Bible when I stepped into that parlor.

Now the voice of whoever had poisoned the air with the word "niggers" came through loud and clear.

"I wish the niggers who ran up north would just stay up north and mind their own business. I wish they'd quit poisoning the minds of the good colored people with all this hate and nonsense."

Someone else, with an exasperated sigh, said, "It's like that wretched War Between the States is happening all over again. If it ain't one group fighting against the South, it's another."

There was silence, then the sobs returned. "Why does everyone hate us so much?" she said. "Southerners are the most hospitable and kindest people in this country. But they treat us like criminals."

Sofas creaked. Feet shuffled. "There, theres" followed.

The only criminals I knew of were Roy Bryant and J. W. Milam, and an all-white jury had set them free. I shook my head and willed my feet to take me to the kitchen—away from the voices of the Cackling Church Club. I'd had enough of the poison they were dishing out. It was making me sick.

Chapter Three

The thing I hated most about helping Ma Pearl out at Mrs. Robinson's house was coming back to my own. From the moment dust began settling on my worn-out shoes as I trudged up the path until the moment I entered our front room filled with Mrs. Robinson's castoffs, my heart felt sick.

As I crossed our splintered porch that evening, anger rose from the depths of my soul. It made no sense that we labored from sunup until sunset in those cotton fields from early spring till late fall, and Mr. Robinson was the only one who had something to show for it.

Rows of pecan trees lined the paved road leading to his home, while a lonely twisted oak, its roots snaking every which way, shaded our grassless front yard. And the house he allowed us to live in, while larger than the houses of a few folks we knew, was still no more than a shack—with no running water, electricity in only one room, and an outside toilet where you constantly swatted flies while doing your business. There wasn't even a sink in the kitchen where we could wash the dishes. Which reminded me of one thing I was grateful for—my hands weren't chafed from lye soap. For her dishes, Mrs. Robinson used a creamy, *liquid* soap, called Joy. The radio advertisement was right: my hands really did feel good immersed in Joy's lotion-soft suds, but that didn't mean I did the dishes "with joy" as the radio announcer so proudly proclaimed I should.

Luckily, at my own house, doing dishes was no longer my concern. With my aunt Ruthie and her brood of five living with us for the past month, housework was how she earned their keep. I was glad she was finally away from Slow John, that evil drunkard husband of hers, but I was not so glad for the extra bodies taking up the small space that already felt cramped.

From the porch I could hear Aunt Ruthie's children through the screen door. Four-year-old Mary Lee and two-year-old Alice chased each other, giggling as always. The boys, seven-year-old Lil' John and six-year-old Virgil, were probably out back with Fred Lee, making themselves useful one way or another. And the baby, little Abigail, for once wasn't screaming from an ear infection or some other ailment.

But once they heard Ma Pearl's heavy footsteps dragging across the porch, they would all grow quiet. I knew that when I opened that screen door to the front room I'd find them sitting as still as the paintings on Mrs. Robinson's walls.

It should have been Aunt Ruthie who ran and hid when

Ma Pearl approached, considering how much Ma Pearl complained about her, always finding fault where there was none. Aunt Ruthie did her best with what she had, but Ma Pearl was never satisfied. The dishes were never washed fast enough. The floor was never swept thoroughly enough. And her oversize bloomers were never bleached white enough. Aunt Ruthie was, after all, having to care for her own children while trying to keep Ma Pearl's house spotless. If Ma Pearl wanted to work someone, she should have taken Queen out of school. She wouldn't be allowed to finish anyway once folks noticed that she was in the family way. Of course, even though Ma Pearl claimed a seventh grade education was more than I needed, she herself knew that finishing high school was the better option for any Negro who had the opportunity. This is why she was trying her best to keep her favorite grandchild—Queen—in school, and her least favorite grandchild—me—out.

With Papa gone to Arkansas, it had been a torturously long weekend for the rest of us left to Ma Pearl's wrath. Later that evening I was so glad to see Reverend Jenkins's car pull up with Papa in it that I almost ran to it and hugged it. But I was too tired to heave myself off the edge of the front porch. So I just sat there, legs swaying back and forth beneath the raised porch, with absolutely no concern for what critters might be lurking below it. I waved wearily as Papa, Reverend Jenkins, and Hallelujah emerged from the Buick. The looks on their faces said they were as weary as I.

They should have returned to Stillwater on Sunday, after the funeral. But Reverend Jenkins had called his sister Bertha to get word to Ma Pearl that they would be staying in Blytheville until today. Some kind of emergency had come up, and it required Reverend Jenkins's attention.

Hallelujah, clad in creased khakis and a soft yellow shirt, walked ahead of Papa and Reverend Jenkins. His penny loafers tread softly over the grass-bare yard as he strolled toward me.

"How was Arkansas?" I asked when he plopped beside me on the edge of the porch.

Hallelujah let out a tired puff of air and removed his fedora from his head. He wiped sweat from his face even though the evening air had a slight chill. His expression told me he was searching for something clever to say. After a moment he frowned and said wryly, "Separate, but not equal."

Though he was frowning, I couldn't help but laugh. "Separate, but not equal" had become our own little saying when white folks in Stillwater started acting even crazier after the Emmett Till murder trial. We couldn't understand why they were so upset. It was the Negro who had lost. Yet somehow they still felt offended that there had ever been the need for the trial in the first place, like that trial somehow signified that the northern Negroes and the NAACP really could make a change in Mississippi. They may have killed Emmett Till, and his murderers might have even gotten away with it, but somehow it still left them ruffled and nervous.

I noticed that Hallelujah still hadn't smiled. He held his fedora in his hands and stared at the ground. It was then that I noticed the looks on Papa's and Reverend Jenkins's faces as they climbed the steps to the porch. When they had entered through the screen door to the parlor, I asked Hallelujah what was going on.

His forehead creased, but he remained silent.

Back in July when he turned fourteen, I thought of how Papa described him as "fourteen going on forty." Yet even then, he still had a fun side to him. But after he witnessed that horrible trial back in September, it seemed his playful spirit had nearly disappeared.

I was hoping it would soon return. I wanted the old Hallelujah back.

I didn't prod him about what was going on. Instead, I put a little space between us, leaned my back against a porch post, and placed my feet upon the porch. I crossed my arms over my chest while I rested my head against the post and closed my eyes. The weariness of the day seemed to seep out of my body and into the cool November air. I needed something to pull the misery that Mrs. Robinson and her church friends had placed in me out.

But just as a nearby whippoorwill began her evening song, Hallelujah decided to speak. "Your cousin David was in jail. That's why we stayed till today. Preacher had to meet with some NAACP members. They had to bail him out."

I bolted upright. "Mule? Uncle Charlie's son? What happened?"

Hallelujah's expression darkened, but he didn't answer me.

The look on his face made my stomach flip. If the NAACP was involved, I knew my cousin had to be in serious trouble. While I had no idea what had happened, just the thought of my cousin being in jail frightened me. David, or Mule, as we called him, had gotten that name because he was stubborn. Born that way, according to Ma Pearl. Took his own sweet time coming out of his mama, nearly killing her.

He also carried a pistol. So thoughts about what he might have done sent shivers up my arms.

"What happened?" I asked again, my throat going dry.

Hallelujah sighed and shook his head. "He punched a white man in the face."

Blood rushed to my head. It throbbed as Hallelujah continued, "David—Mule—used to work for the man, at his restaurant. He fired Mule but still owed him money. Mule's story is that he went to the man's house to get his money, and the man attacked him."

I cringed. "Please don't tell me that the man said Mule attacked him instead."

Hallelujah shook his head. "He didn't." With a frustrated sigh, he said, "No. Mule didn't hit him *then*. He thought he'd pay him back another way. He decided to go to the man's restaurant and waltz right into the dining room and sit down."

"What!"

Hallelujah nodded. "Yep."

"Mule is so stupid," I said through gritted teeth.

"When the man asked him to leave, Mule got up, punched the man in the face, and tore out of there faster than a hound on a hunt."

"God help us," I whispered.

"That's what caused your uncle Charlie to have a heart attack. When the sheriff came to the house to arrest Mule, your uncle Charlie just slumped over and died."

"When Papa got word that Uncle Charlie had died, nobody told him what happened. Just that his heart gave out while he was sitting at home eating his supper."

"I guess they didn't wanna risk Mr. Carter's heart giving out, too."

I shook my head. "This is horrible."

Hallelujah frowned and stared at the ground. "That's not all."

My heart took a dive.

"They beat him up pretty bad in jail. Broke most of his ribs and his right jaw. His eye was still swollen shut when we saw him. That's why the NAACP had to get him out. He's lucky to be alive."

"What's gonna happen now?"

"He got charged with trespassing and assault and battery. Preacher said there'll be a trial."

"Is Mule safe? What if they come after him while he's out of jail?"

"He's hidden. But it's up to him to stay put and stay out of trouble."

I groaned. "I can't believe this is happening. How could Mule do something so dumb? How could he just walk right into the man's restaurant and hit him in the face?"

Hallelujah clenched his teeth. "He said he was fed up. Now he's *beat-up. And* your uncle Charlie is dead."

A sharp pain hit my stomach when I thought about the one person who was probably suffering the most—Aunt Mildred, Mule's mama. "How's Aunt Mildred holding up?"

Hallelujah frowned and shook his head. "Terrible."

"It's a shame that a white man in Mississippi can kill a

Negro and be set free. But all a colored man has to do is hit a white man and he gets beat up in jail."

"The NAACP hired him a lawyer. Hopefully he'll at least get a fair trial."

My mouth twisted into a frown. "Speaking of trials, I heard something at the Robinsons' today. I'm not real sure, but I think they were talking about Roy Bryant and his brother. They said something about 'making those boys go back to court.'"

Hallelujah rolled his eyes. "It's not a trial. A grand jury will decide whether there will *be* a trial for kidnapping."

"For kidnapping Emmett Till?"

Hallelujah nodded.

"After they've already been set free for killing him?"

"Yep."

"When is this court thing?"

"Wednesday."

"This Wednesday?"

"Yep."

"And you didn't tell me about it?"

Hallelujah shrugged. "What's to tell? The case will go before a grand jury who already knows they kidnapped Emmett Till. The grand jury will say there's not enough evidence and dismiss the whole thing, making a mockery of the NAACP and all their efforts once again. Bryant and Milam will never see the inside of a prison for killing or kidnapping Emmett Till."

I grunted. "And who knows what will happen with poor Mule just for punching a white man, *once*."

"Mm-hmm," Hallelujah said, nodding.

"Did you also know that they're integrating schools in Arkansas?" I asked.

Hallelujah's forehead creased. "You talking about Hoxie?"

"You knew?"

"Yeah."

"How come you didn't tell me that either?"

Hallelujah shrugged. "Forgot."

"How could you forget something so important?"

"Important?" Hallelujah scoffed. "They only integrated because they're too broke to segregate. Now, if it'd been a big city like Little Rock, that would be important. That would be good news, like Topeka, Kansas."

"Humph," I said. "The Cackling Church Club clucked about it like Chicken Little, like the sky was falling, and the end was near."

"The Cackling Church Club?"

I grinned. "That's what I call Mrs. Robinson's Bible study group."

"I'd like to be a fly on the wall and listen in on them sometimes myself," said Hallelujah.

I told him what Mrs. Robinson and her friend had said about colored children not being smart enough to attend the same school as white children.

His face flushed with anger. "So I guess they never heard of Dr. T. R. M. Howard right up in Mound Bayou?" he said. "Do they think he became a surgeon by accident? He had to attend medical school just like any white doctor."

Nodding in agreement, I said, "And if they'd rewrite those history texts like Miss Johnson suggested last year in seventh grade, then they'd know that colored people were artists and writers and inventors and explorers and a whole bunch of other important things just like white people."

Hallelujah rolled his eyes and said, "We'll only get the truth when we write our own history books."

"Mrs. Jamison, *at least,* said she was happy that schools are integrating. She thinks Stillwater should integrate too."

Hallelujah nodded. "The Jamisons are good people."

I raised a brow. "'Good white peoples,' as Ma Pearl would say?"

Hallelujah frowned. "No. Just good people."

We fell into silence for a moment and let Hallelujah's words just sit there. It was kind of refreshing to refer to people as just good people, and not colored or white. Ma Pearl often referred to the Robinsons as good white people because they gave us things that were no longer of use to them and because they treated us better than some other white landowners treated the colored folk living on their land. The Robinsons, in turn, referred to Ma Pearl and Papa as good colored people because they didn't cause trouble and because Papa tended to his cotton with care even though he was not the one who benefited from it and Ma Pearl tended to Mrs. Robinson's every need without complaint. They claimed them good colored people because they didn't aspire to be more than Negroes should aspire to be.

Hallelujah began speaking again about Hoxie, Arkansas. "Hoxie integrated in the summer," he said. "We had our own worries at the time. Bigger worries—like Levi getting killed, for one."

Levi Jackson. I leaned my back against the porch post and let the name soak in. Levi Jackson. Just turned twenty-one. Registered to vote. Run off the road and shot. Dead. His parents' dream of him being the first person in their family to graduate college dead, too. Whole family packed up and moved to Detroit shortly after his funeral.

"Lamar Smith," Hallelujah said. "Dead. And nobody's in jail to pay for the crime."

"And Emmett Till," I added, cringing.

Hallelujah nodded. "Murderers brought to trial. Acquitted. All in one summer."

Chills crept over me.

"And before all them, Reverend Lee was killed in May, and nobody was ever arrested," said Hallelujah. "Now watch your cousin Mule end up going to jail and sitting there until the sun turns as white as the moon, just for *hitting* a white man."

"If they even bother with a trial," I muttered.

"They'll have a trial. It's the law."

Hallelujah's words hung in the chilly evening air as heavy as the scent of honeysuckle on a hot day. *It's the law.* Since when did any laws, except the Jim Crow laws, apply to the treatment of Negroes? If it hadn't been for the NAACP, Mule could've been dead at that very moment—his body floating somewhere in an Arkansas river.

I didn't realize I was frowning until Hallelujah said, "Don't let your face freeze like that."

I tried to relax my face, but I couldn't. It had begun to match my heart.

Chapter Four

THURSDAY, NOVEMBER 10

THE DAY AFTER A GRAND JURY REFUSED TO HOLD ROY Bryant and J. W. Milam accountable for kidnapping Emmett Till, it seemed the world was about to explode, especially in our little colored school.

Despite how many times our teacher, Miss Hill, asked them to, the students would not calm down. And it was Hallelujah who had incited them. Earlier that morning he had gotten permission from the ninth-grade teacher Miss Wilson to come over and speak to the eighth-grade students regarding a history project on Abraham Lincoln and the Emancipation Proclamation. I knew from the devious look on his face when he entered the room that he had something else in mind. Instead, he educated us on how it was time for colored folks to demand their civil rights. I doubt any of us would have known a thing about what the grand jury had said if it hadn't been for him. I doubt any of us would have known what a grand jury was, for that matter, had it not been for Hallelujah.

A grand jury, he told us, is like a regular jury—twelve

average people randomly selected to determine whether there is enough evidence for a case to go to trial. And with Roy Bryant and J. W. Milam, it didn't matter that, the Monday morning after Reverend Mose Wright told the sheriff his great-nephew had been taken, the sheriff arrested the two and locked them away in jail. Nor did it matter that they both had admitted they "took the boy." But I guess since they claimed they only "gave him a good talking to and released him," their twelve peers didn't see anything criminal about what they had done.

"How can they not try them for kidnapping?" Hallelujah demanded, banging his fist on an already beat-up desk — a castoff from the white school on the other side of Stillwater. "They admitted it during the first trial. Those murderers should be tried, found guilty, and sent to prison for what they did. Instead, they get to go right back to living their lives, making money off colored folks — the very folks they just made a mockery of."

Miss Hill, a tall, wide-hipped, narrow-waisted woman with a wispy voice that didn't match her size, stood before the students and asked us not to discuss anything further about the Emmett Till murder inside her classroom.

She asked Hallelujah to leave.

But regardless of how much she fidgeted and twirled the

gold-toned bracelet she always wore around her left wrist, Hallelujah would not leave and the students would not stop whispering. They whispered about Emmett Till, the trial, and all the marching going on, even in places like New York City. All of this was information Hallelujah had fed them. And if it hadn't been for the fact that his father, Reverend Clyde B. Jenkins the Second, was the English teacher at the high school, Miss Hill might have asked some of the other boys to throw him right out of her class.

But I don't think even that would have worked. Hallelujah had created his own little uprising in our class that morning, and everyone seemed eager to hear what he had to say.

"Reverend Mose Wright risked his life coming down here again to testify," he said. "He could have been lynched just like his nephew. And a Leflore County grand jury still found those murderers not guilty. How? Please tell me how."

We all knew how. But nobody said a word. Once again, Roy Bryant and J. W. Milam, like schoolchildren on a play-ground, had been brought before a group of their peers, this time to determine whether or not they should be brought to trial for kidnapping Emmett Till. To me, it was kind of like what Papa called closing the barn door after the cow had al-ready gotten out. If their peers wouldn't send them to prison for murder, why would they send them there for kidnapping?

Again, the justice system in Mississippi simply wanted to appease (or maybe even tease) northern Negroes and the NAACP.

Miss Hill wrung her hands. "Jenkins," she said nervously. (Jenkins is what the teachers called Hallelujah, since his real name was Clyde Bernard Jenkins the Third.) "Please respect my authority as the teacher in this classroom and leave. You said you wanted to speak about a history project, and that's why I allowed you to take time away from my prepared lesson. I did not give you permission to speak about a trial, and I'm sure Miss Wilson didn't either."

Without a word, Hallelujah dropped his hands to his sides and marched to the door. When he opened it, Miss Hill sighed and relaxed her shoulders. But I noticed that her hands shook when she picked up the worn history text from her desk. As soon as she balanced the open book in one hand and began flipping through it with the other, Hallelujah turned back and stared at the class. "I think we should take a vote," he said.

Miss Hill tilted her head to one side. "A vote?"

Hallelujah nodded. "Yes, a vote." He shut the door and faced the class. "All in favor of discussing this mockery of a trial, raise your hands."

At first, no hands went up. Then slowly, one after another,

fourteen hands, including mine, came up no higher than our faces.

With a grin, Hallelujah turned to Miss Hill. "The people have voted. We would like to openly discuss this matter further."

Miss Hill took a deep breath and let it out. "I don't think that's a good idea," she said. She glanced at the door. Her eyes, disproportionately large compared with the rest of her facial features, revealed her fear.

But her nervousness didn't stop the whispers. The students began talking, not only about Emmett Till but about Levi Jackson's murder only a month before, in July. As the whispers grew louder and into full-out talking, Hallelujah called the class to order.

Miss Hill dropped the history book onto the desk and, eyes brimming with tears, rushed from the room. Hallelujah did not seem bothered as he stood before the class and addressed us. "As I was saying before, a grand jury has decided there will be no trial. There will be no more wasting of their time and money for this kind of nonsense—the nonsense of bringing to trial white men for the killing or kidnapping of a Negro. And you know why?"

Hallelujah paused for a response, but there was none.

"Because white men have been kidnapping men of color

for ages, beginning with our ancestors from Africa. So of course they don't consider it a crime. They see us as less than human. Not even as good as a hog. As a matter of fact, they probably would try a white man for stealing a hog. But never for taking a Negro from his home in the middle of the night.

"And I bet a white man would spend time in jail for shooting someone's dog. But never a Negro—someone's family member. Even wild animals get protection and can't be shot outside of hunting season. But in Mississippi, it's always open season on the Negro."

Murmurs filled the room.

"And just what is we s'pose to do 'bout this?" came a voice from the back of the room.

I turned to find that the person speaking was a boy who was supposedly a cousin of mine, from my daddy's side of my family—the Banks family. Except his last name was Cooper. And like Fred Lee and me, he carried his grandparents' last name rather than his father's. Also, like Fred Lee and me, his mama no longer walked the soil of the Mississippi Delta. Instead, she had migrated to California, leaving the boy, James "Shorty" Cooper, behind to be raised by his grandparents, Raymond and Velma Dean Cooper.

Shorty, who at sixteen was the oldest student in the eighth grade, cocked his head and raised a brow at Hallelujah. "What we go'n do 'bout it, Preacha' Boy?"

Hallelujah, with his hands crossed over his chest and his feet firmly planted and shoulder-width apart, mimicked his father's preaching stance. "I say we do what the people in Chicago and New York are doing. I say we march."

"March?" several voices echoed. Then the whispers started up again, slowly at first, before they escalated into discernible words. *Crazy. Fool. Done. Lost. His. Mind.*

"What good is marching?" asked Shorty. "White folks is shootin'. I say we shoot back."

Suddenly, voices exploded. Angry words jumbled together, but names came out loud and clear. *Reverend Lee. Levi Jackson. Lamar Smith. Emmett Till.*

"Kill them 'fo they kill us!" Shorty shouted over the commotion. "Them dirty dogs done shot down a sixty-three-year-old man and a fourteen-year-old boy. Who go'n be next? Somebody's granmama?"

The room grew quiet, so quiet that all we heard were birds chirping through the open window.

"You can march all you want," Shorty said, "but I'm pickin' up my grandaddy's shotgun. I ain't lettin' no white man come up in my house like that preacha' did. I ain't go'n wait 'round to git shot. And I sho' ain't go'n march on the street and git gunned out."

Shorty, who once rightfully earned his nickname in his elementary years, was now a head taller than any other boy in the class. His age, too, made him intimidating. But that he couldn't help. He was one of the students who worked the fields and only attended school part of the year, hence he had repeated multiple grades.

I thought about my cousin Mule in Arkansas and how the sheriff came to arrest him. My own heart ached when I envisioned the toll it took on poor Uncle Charlie—his eyes widening, his heart giving out, his shoulders slumping, his head dropping forward. Dead. No bullets required.

What if Mule had used that pistol of his and shot the man who owed him money, instead of just punching him in the face? He'd probably be dead right now himself. They wouldn't have bothered with an arrest, jail, and beating him up. A lynch mob would have hunted him down to string him up instead.

I jumped when the classroom door burst open. Wild-eyed, Miss Hill rushed in. I expected to see one of the male teachers, specifically Reverend Jenkins, following her. Instead, it was the pudgy little white man from the county office. The scowl on his face said he was not happy with the colored children on the other side of town.

Chapter Five

THURSDAY, NOVEMBER 10

WHAT'S THE TROUBLE IN HE'AH?" THE VERY ROUND Mr. Cartwright asked.

Though the room grew quieter than a graveyard, Hallelujah maintained his defiant stance. *Please sit down and pretend you belong in here,* I begged him. I was so scared that my heart felt as if it would thump out of my chest and land bleeding on the floor. It wasn't Mr. Cartwright, the man in charge of making sure everything was okay with the colored schools, who frightened me. It was Hallelujah, and the way he stared him down.

I still had that copy of *Jet* magazine he had shared with me back in September, right before the murder trial. It was securely hidden at the bottom of the cardboard box that held my folded clothes—safe from Ma Pearl's eyes. But I removed it often, studying the photo of Emmett Till almost as much as I did my textbooks. Hallelujah, with his eyes narrowed at Mr. Cartwright, resembled him even more than I thought he had the first time I glanced at the picture.

Though he stared straight at Hallelujah, Mr. Cartwright asked Miss Hill, "This the boy causing the trouble?"

Miss Hill, too chicken to speak, nodded.

Mr. Cartwright fixed his eyes on Hallelujah's face, then let them roll down toward to his feet. They came back up again, slowly, to meet his eyes. Nearly spitting, he asked, "Ain't you Preacher Jenkins's boy?"

Hallelujah returned Mr. Cartwright's steely-eyed stare. "My father is Reverend Clyde B. Jenkins the Second," he said.

When Hallelujah sealed his lips, indicating he had nothing further to say, everyone in the room seemed to suck in air at once. We all knew it was practically a crime for a colored person to address a white person and not end their statement with "sir" or "ma'am."

I jumped when a flock of black birds suddenly took flight from the tree directly outside the window. The noise they made momentarily took attention away from the standoff between Hallelujah and Mr. Cartwright.

Bodies shuffled in their seats.

"Hallelujah is Reverend Jenkins's son, sir," Miss Hill said loudly, emphasizing "sir."

Mr. Cartwright took his eyes off Hallelujah long enough to say to Miss Hill, "I know who he is." Then to Hallelujah he said, "Boy, you tell that pappy of yours that if he wants to keep his job ovah he'ah, he best keep you outta trouble. The school board don't tolerate teachers who cain't control their own offspring."

Hallelujah neither uttered a response nor took his eyes off Mr. Cartwright.

Mr. Cartwright grunted and motioned toward the class. "If he cain't control his own spawn, how can we expect him to control the rest o' these niggers?"

Miss Hill looked as if she might faint.

"You people have developed a false sense of security because of them northern agitators," Mr. Cartwright continued. "That troublemaking N-A-A-C-P."

He stopped, turned his face toward the window, then frowned.

He stood there, for what felt like something close to eternity and stared at the last of the yellow leaves waving in the breeze, clinging to the giant tree.

He finally turned his attention back to the class and said, "You people should appreciate all we do for you." Then, gazing steely-eyed at Hallelujah, he said, "Now git on back to your classroom, boy."

Without lowering his head even one bit, Hallelujah marched toward the door. Even there in the classroom, knowing Mr. Cartwright wouldn't touch him without a lynch mob at his side, I feared for Hallelujah's life. His behavior was what Ma Pearl would have called downright uppity.

"And tell that pappy o' yours that he ain't foolin' nobody," Mr. Cartwright said, grinning slyly. "We know 'bout the meetin's. Let him know we're havin' our meetin's, too."

When they had both left the room, Shorty Cooper confronted Miss Hill. "Why you run 'n fetch Chubby Cartwright?"

Miss Hill fiddled with her bracelet. "I didn't *fetch* him," she said. "He caught me talking to Mr. Bryson in the office and asked me why I was out of my classroom."

"And you couldn't lie?" asked Shorty.

Miss Hill stormed toward the open window. When she reached it, she stared out for a second, then slammed it shut. Abruptly, she turned and fixed her eyes on Shorty. With newfound confidence, she said, "I don't owe you any explanations, James Cooper."

Shorty only snorted, but a girl named Barbara spoke up. "You should've stood up for Hallelujah," she said. She gestured around the room. "We all should have been standing up for him instead of letting Chubby Cartwright wear him down like that. He was only trying to help us be more aware of what's going on around here."

With her forehead creased, Miss Hill narrowed her eyes at Barbara. "I will not tolerate that disrespect in my classroom." She glanced toward the door, then cut her eyes at Shorty. "It's Mr. Cartwright." Then to Barbara, "You know better."

"I know we need to *do* better," said Barbara.

Miss Hill snatched up her history text and said, "None of you will tell me how to run my classroom. I won't lose my job over this nonsense."

Barbara's cousin Dorothy spoke up. "It ain't nonsense," she said. "It's truth. And we need to know about it. Colored folks in the South been asleep long enough. We need to wake up down here."

"Open your books," Miss Hill ordered us, ignoring Dorothy.

"Why?" Shorty challenged.

"This is school," Miss Hill replied curtly. "You came here to learn, not to debate trials. Or to talk about that foolishness going on up north."

With a swift wave of his right hand, Shorty swept the history text off his desk. "I ain't stud'n no mo' lies from white folks. Ain't nothin' in that book 'bout me. One page, talkin' 'bout Abraham Lincoln freein' slaves. And even that been ripped out."

Without a word, Miss Hill marched over and retrieved the book from the floor. She glared at Shorty and said, "Leave." She flared her nostrils and said, "Go on back to the cotton field and be ignorant."

"Ign'ant?" Shorty said with a snort. "You thank 'cause you know the stuff in that book, that make you smart?"

Miss Hill held his stare but said nothing.

Shorty chuckled. The rest of us squirmed. The air in the room had quickly grown stiff with the window closed. But it wasn't nearly as stiff as Miss Hill stood as Shorty spoke his next words.

"You ain't nothin' but a Jim Crow nigga," he said. "You got that college education, but what good it do you? You thank we don't know you work them fields in summertime jest like the rest o' us do?"

He stood. And although Miss Hill was tall, his six-foot frame towered over her. Shorty bent forward. "Chop, chop, chop," he said, as he pretended to hoe a field. "Got my college education, but the white man don't pay me 'nuff to make a livin'. Got to chop his cotton jest like the rest o' dese dumb niggas if I wants to eat."

"Get out," Miss Hill said.

"We hold these truths to be self-evident," Shorty said, his face hard. "All mens is not created equal. The Negro ain't endowed by his Creator with them in-ale-li-en-able rights that book talk about. That ain't my history," he said, nodding toward the book in Miss Hill's hand. "That story belong to the white man."

Chapter Six

FRIDAY, NOVEMBER 11

Its time for somthng new," Shorty's note read. "I need yor help. Meat me afta scool."

Without a word, Shorty had pressed the note into my hand during lunchtime and quickly walked away. What made him think I could stay after school? For one, Ma Pearl never allowed me to stay in town after school for any reason. And two, we lived eight miles out. I would have to walk home if I missed my ride with Uncle Ollie.

Yet as I sat through science, the last class of the day, totally uninterested in the life cycle of a frog, I couldn't help but consider Shorty's note. It's time for something new. What did that mean? And why did he think I could help?

Not only was I curious about his plan, I also wanted desperately to ask him about something else—whether we were truly related, and if so, whether he knew anything about my daddy, Johnny Lee Banks. Through school, I had known Shorty for years. But except for a nod or two of acknowledgment, we had never really spoken. Perhaps it was time we did.

By the time class was dismissed, I had come up with a plan to stay after school. I knew Ma Pearl would never believe I needed help with my schoolwork, nor would she go for me staying late to help one of my teachers. So I volunteered my brother, Fred Lee. My plan was risky, but I was willing to take a chance if it meant I might get to know more about my daddy.

"Don't worry about cleaning the blackboards or sweeping and mopping, Mrs. Washington," I said while the rest of the class filed out of the room. "Me and my brother Fred Lee can do that."

Mrs. Washington, one of the most refined Negroes I had ever met, frowned and peered at me over her wire-rimmed glasses. "My brother Fred Lee and I," she corrected me.

I nodded. "Yes, ma'am. My brother Fred Lee and I is what I meant." I knew that, and I don't know why I allowed my grammar to slip around Mrs. Washington. She could embarrass a soul worse than Ma Pearl could.

Mrs. Washington smiled slightly, which was rare—the smile, that is, not the slightness of it. She was dressed in a navy blue skirt paired with a silky beige blouse. Her feet sported blue high heels that matched her skirt. She was definitely not dressed to perform her janitorial services, which the school board did not provide but required of the individual teachers.

"What makes you think I clean this room at the end of the day?" she asked.

I glanced around the room. "Somebody does. It's always clean."

"I have some girls who come in after school and take care of my room for me."

I felt like a plum fool. I hadn't noticed that Mrs. Washington's hands were just as nice as Mrs. Robinson's. A bright red polish even coated her nails.

"If you're interested in helping them," she continued, "feel free. But I can't pay you."

"Pay?" I asked, my brows raised. "I wasn't expecting to be paid, ma'am. I was volunteering."

This time it was Mrs. Washington who raised her brows. "Oh," she said. Then, "Hmmm. Volunteering?"

"Yes, ma'am."

I realized the time was running out as we stood there debating paid work against volunteer work. Fred Lee would be waiting for me near the front door of the school, and Shorty would be waiting for me at the side exit. I needed to get to Fred Lee and convince him to come clean Mrs. Washington's room while I met up with Shorty.

Two girls entered the classroom. I recognized them—one from the eighth grade class, the other from the ninth. They were sisters who lived in town with their mama and their elderly grandparents. From what I was told, their mama did washing and ironing for various white women in Stillwater.

"Althea. Aretha," Mrs. Washington called out to the girls. "I won't need you to clean the classroom today." She glanced at me, sized me up, and said to Althea and Aretha, "Come back on Monday. I'll let you know whether I still need you then."

Both girls looked a bit shocked, but neither said a word as they backed out of the door.

Mrs. Washington stuffed papers into a black satchel. "I'll determine whether I want to use you and your brother after I see whether you can do a better job than those two," she said, nodding toward the door. "You did say volunteer, right?"

I swallowed the lump in my throat. I had no plans to clean Mrs. Washington's classroom every evening. I had enough chores waiting for me at home. "With all due respect, Mrs. Washington, my brother and I can only clean your room today."

Mrs. Washington paused her paper stuffing and pursed her lips.

I hated that look.

She removed her glasses and peered steely-eyed at me. "I just sent those girls on their way because you offered to clean my room at no cost to me."

I stammered. "I—I meant today only."

"Why today?" she asked.

I was already about to go home and lie to Ma Pearl. Now I was being forced to lie to Mrs. Washington as well. Because I certainly couldn't tell her the truth. She, like Ma Pearl, would only think the worst if I told her I needed to meet Shorty Cooper after school.

I sighed and said, "It's not for me. It's for my brother Fred Lee."

As if she already doubted me, Mrs. Washington raised an eyebrow.

Oh, what a tangled web we weave, when first we practice to deceive. How many times had I heard Reverend Jenkins say that during a sermon? More than I cared to count.

"Well," I said, still fumbling for words. "He doesn't want to go straight home. He—he got in trouble this morning," I blurted when the lie began forming in my head. "He figures the longer he's gone, the better chance our grandma will forget about the whupping she promised he'd get as soon as we got back."

Mrs. Washington began shoving more papers into her satchel. The only word she had for me was "Umm-hmmm." And I could tell from the way she said it that she neither believed me nor cared. She only wanted the free cleaning for the afternoon.

"So Monday I'm back to paying Aretha and Althea," she said after her satchel was sufficiently stuffed.

I swallowed all my lies with one gulp and nodded.

Mrs. Washington snatched up the satchel and glared at me. "You and your brother clean the room today," she said. "But don't ever waste my time and resources like this again. Understand?"

With shame rising in my face, I stared at the floor and uttered, "Yes, ma'am."

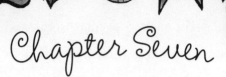

Chapter Seven

FRIDAY, NOVEMBER 11

BY THE TIME I CONVINCED FRED LEE TO CLEAN MRS. Washington's classroom, and by the time Mrs. Washington trusted us enough to leave her room so I could escape as well, Shorty, with the toe of his worn brown shoe, was snuffing out what looked to be his fourth cigarette, based on the butts already scattered on the ground.

And the look on his face said he was just about ready to head home. He squinted one-eyed at me and asked, "What took you so long, girl?"

The air was chilly, but sweat rolled down my back just the same. And it was not just the fact that I had spun a web of lies that made me nervous. It was the fact that I was only thirteen and was standing under a sugar gum tree in the schoolyard with a boy who was sixteen. A boy who was smoking cigarettes, or doing the devil's business as Ma Pearl would say. Of course, it didn't seem to bother her that Papa pretended to smoke a pipe. Nor did it bother her that his mama, Grandma Mandy actually did smoke one. I was no more than about five or six years old, but I could still remember the sweet scent of the smoke from the Prince Albert tobacco floating from the front porch where Grandma Mandy smoked every evening.

But the cigarettes that Shorty smoked smelled nothing like the Prince Albert tobacco. A thick fog lingered in the air, and I had to only half breathe in order to keep from choking. My stomach churned when he pulled a pack of Kools from his shirt pocket and shook one out.

Using the bark on the tree, he struck a match and lit his cigarette. "You don't mind, do you?" he asked, the cigarette dangling from his mouth.

I shook my head. But I did mind. The scent was sickening. The man on the radio claimed cigarettes could freshen your breath. "As cool and as clean as a breath of fresh air," he said. "Your mouth feels clean, your throat refreshed." But I don't know how that was possible seeing how horrible that smoke smelled when Shorty blew it from his mouth.

Shorty inhaled deeply, his cheeks going in so far, it's a wonder he didn't pass out. After a moment of sucking in whatever there was to suck in from the cigarette, he exhaled, releasing a stream of gray into the cool November air.

"What did you need to talk to me about?" I asked. "I can't stay long. My brother's cleaning Mrs. Washington's classroom, then we have to head home. It's a long walk. We need to get there before dark."

Shorty nodded toward a beat-up black pickup, its color more rust than black. "I'll give you a ride."

I nodded, and Shorty continued. "You good friends with Preacha' Boy, ain't you?"

"Yeah. Hallelujah and I are friends."

Shorty flicked ashes from the cigarette and chuckled. "That boy stupid as the day long."

My forehead creased. "Hallelujah is the smartest boy I know," I said in his defense.

"Book smart," Shorty replied. "He know them books a'right. But he don't know nothin' 'bout real life."

I hadn't risked getting a beating by Ma Pearl just to stand there and listen to Shorty put down Hallelujah. "I'm going back inside to help my brother so we can get on home," I said.

When I turned to leave, Shorty grabbed my arm. His hand was rough and callused, probably from gripping a hoe since he was a child like me.

"Sorry," he said, sounding like he really meant it. "I shouldn'a said that."

I grimaced and stared at his grimy fingers gripping my arm.

He let go.

He kicked at a bed of brown and yellow leaves piled at the base of the tree, then sat on the ground. With his cigarette-free hand, he motioned me to join him.

"I'll stand," I said. It was bad enough I was out there with him in the first place, so I certainly didn't want to risk someone seeing us sitting under a tree together. Especially if that someone happened to be Reverend Jenkins. Or Miss Johnson, my teacher from seventh grade. She always warned us girls to stay away from certain types of boys. I didn't really know what kind of boy Shorty was, but puffing away on that cigarette right outside the school didn't give him the image of a good boy.

"So what did you want to talk to me about?" I asked. "Your note said it was time for something new, and you need my help. It didn't say anything about putting down my best friend."

Shorty raised his eyebrows. "Best friend, huh?"

"Since we were little."

Shorty smirked. "Don't know what to think of a fella whose best friend is a girl."

Again I turned to leave.

Shorty quickly apologized. "Look, I'm sorry." He shook his head. "Things jest seem so easy for him. Got his daddy here teachin'. Got that fancy Buick to ride in. Them fancy clothes like some city boy from up nawth. Fancy way o' talkin'," he said, frowning.

"You're jealous of Hallelujah?"

Shorty scoffed. "I ain't jealous o' that joker."

"Well, maybe you ought to get to know folks before you judge them," I said. "Hallelujah's had a hard life too."

"Hard life? What that clown know 'bout a hard life?"

"For one, he doesn't have a mama."

"I ain't got one neither."

"His is dead."

"Mine's too," said Shorty. "Far as I'm concerned."

"Your mama's in California. Just like mine is in Chicago. They ain't dead in the grave. We can still see them."

"When the last time you see'd yo' mama?"

"July," I answered curtly.

"And that 'bout go'n be yo' last time. I ain't see'd my mama since I was two. Since the day she hopped in my uncle's car and caught a ride to California."

"You haven't seen your mama in fourteen years?"

Shorty placed his cigarette between his lips and sucked in his cheeks for a real long time. When he finally blew out a stream of smoke, he said, "Like I said, she dead to me."

Shorty cleared a spot of leaves, then ground the cigarette into the dirt until the tip stopped burning. "What you know 'bout that marchin' they doin' up nawth?"

"Only what Hallelujah told me, and what I read in *Jet* magazine."

Shorty's face lit up. "You see'd one o' them?"

"A few," I answered. "Reverend Jenkins gets a copy every week. Hallelujah sometimes brings them by the house so I can keep up with what's going on with colored folks outside of Leflore County, Mississippi."

"You thank I could git holt to one?"

"I'm sure Hallelujah would bring you a copy if you asked."

Shorty shook his head. "Fellas like him don't 'sociate with fellas like me."

"What's that supposed to mean?"

"High-class Negroes don't talk to low-class Negroes."

I threw up my hands. "There you go again, judging folks. I'm leaving."

Shorty leaped up. "Wait."

I flinched before he could grab my arm.

"So this marchin' that's goin' on," he said, "Preacha' Boy thank we should do it too, huh?"

"Stop calling him Preacha' Boy."

Shorty sat back down, cross-legged, on the ground. He huffed out a puff of air. "What good it doin' the Negro in the South to have a bunch a peoples in the Nawth walkin' 'round shoutin' words with no meaning? How that go'n change some-thin' in Miss'sippi?"

I didn't have an answer, so I asked him a question. "What do you want me to do? Why did you ask me to meet you?"

"Talk to Preacha'—I mean yo' friend."

"And tell him what?"

Shorty shook his head. "I don' need you to tell him nothin'. I need you to tell me what he sayin'."

"Why can't you talk to him yourself? Why do you need me as your go-between?"

Shorty frowned. "I told you. He ain't go'n talk to me."

"Have you tried?"

"Don't hafta. I already know he won't have nothin' to do with somebody like me. Folks like him don' view folks like me no higher than a slave, takin' care o' the white man's cotton."

"I live on a white man's cotton plantation, and Hallelujah's friends with me."

"You different. You smart."

"So?"

Shorty scowled. "He know you ain't go'n always be out there on Robinson's place. Him and his daddy both know you go'n move on one day."

"The Jenkinses don't class themselves like that."

Shorty snorted. "You got some learnin' to do, girl."

"So what's your plan, Shorty Cooper? How you gonna

change things? How you gonna keep Negroes in Mississippi from getting killed?"

Shorty stood again and leaned against the tree. "Fight back. That's what we need to do."

"When you say *fight*, you don't actually mean like with fists, do you?"

"Fists, feets, even guns if that what it take to git these peckerwoods to leave us alone."

My heart raced. Fists. Feet. *Guns.* "You really talking about shooting someone?"

"That's exactly what I'm talkin' 'bout," Shorty said. He clenched his hands into fists. "Kill one o' them. Show 'em what it feel like to be scared all the time."

Now my heart threatened to beat right out of my chest. "I don't think Hallelujah would go along with any plan that involved killing people." I said. "And neither would I."

Shorty squinted at me. "You say you reads them *Jet* magazines, don't ya?"

I nodded.

"Then you know 'bout that Negro doctor in Mound Bayou."

"Dr. T. R. M. Howard," I said.

"That's him," Shorty said, nodding. "I heard he said somethin' 'bout Negroes go'n start fightin' back if white folks don't stop slaughterin' us like hogs."

"Where'd you hear that?"

Shorty shrugged. "Overheard a coupla teachers talkin' 'bout it when Hill kicked me out the classroom yesterday."

"I remember reading that in the last magazine that Hallelujah let me borrow. Dr. Howard said that we would only take so much before we start to fight back."

"He right," Shorty said. "And you know what happen in a war?"

I swallowed and said, "People die."

Shorty frowned. "And I'm go'n do my best to make sho' I ain't one o' the dead ones."

"You still haven't said what you need me for," I said. "I don't plan on shooting anyone. And I sure don't want to die anytime soon."

"I don' need you to fight. I need you to be smart. I need you to keep me in the know. Tell me what's goin' on. Tell me what all these NAACP peoples talkin' 'bout. What they plan on doin'."

"What makes you think I have all this information?"

"You friends with Lil' Jenkins."

"So?"

Shorty sneered. "I don' care what you say. Colored folks like them Jenkinses class theyselves. But they see somethin' in you." He nodded and added, "I see it too."

Before I could respond, the side door to the school swung

open. Fred Lee, book satchel in hand, stepped outside, shielding his face from what was left of the sunshine with his free hand.

"My brother's finished," I said. "We gotta go home. You still giving us a ride?"

"Yeah," Shorty said, his face set as if he was now sorry he'd mentioned it.

I still hadn't asked him anything about my daddy. "We can finish talking on the way," I said. "We live eight miles out. You can drop us off at the seventh mile. We'll walk the rest of the way."

Shorty shook his head. "Cain't talk with yo' brother in the truck. Don't know who side he on."

"Side?" I asked. "He's colored. What side you think he's on?"

Shorty snorted. "Lotta us on the wrong side—tryin' to stay in good with the whites."

"Fred Lee ain't like that," I said. My voice was sure but my heart wasn't. How was I supposed to know whose side my brother was on? I supposed none of us would really know that answer until the time came, until we were tested.

"And if he on our side," Shorty said, "is he on the marchin' side, or is he on the fightin' side?"

When Fred Lee approached us, we stopped talking. "Ready to go?" I asked him.

"Been ready," he answered, glaring at Shorty.

"Shorty's giving us a ride." I pointed my thumb toward the raggedy black truck.

Fred Lee stared at it as if he doubted it would get us out of the schoolyard.

"It run," Shorty said.

"I know it do," Fred Lee answered. "You drove it here."

I touched Shorty's arm and whispered, "You wouldn't happen to have any money, would you?"

"Lil' bit," Shorty answered, looking confused. Without asking questions but with his forehead creased in one, he fished around in his pants pocket—which sounded like it held many keys—and found some coins. He dropped three quarters into my outstretched hand. "That's all I have."

My face lit up. "This is good enough!"

Shorty frowned. "Didn't know I was go'n hafta pay you."

"You didn't," I said. "The money's to keep me and my brother from getting in trouble with our grandma."

Shorty shook his head. He looked even more confused.

Chapter Eight

FRIDAY, NOVEMBER 11

IF SHORTY'S TRUCK HADN'T BROKEN DOWN, WE WOULD
have made it home at a decent time. But since Shorty's truck
did break down, Fred Lee and I ended up walking nearly five
miles instead of one. By the time we reached the front yard,
the sun was setting and Ma Pearl was waiting for us on the
porch. The black strap of terror, the thick leather strap she
used for discipline, swung threateningly from her right hand.

"Where the devil y'all been?" she yelled from the porch.

I was exhausted from the walk, but I hurried along anyway. Poor Fred Lee. Not only had he walked five miles, but
he had also cleaned Mrs. Washington's classroom. Even the
sight of the black strap of terror couldn't give him the energy
to walk faster.

I climbed up the steps and said, "Me and Fred Lee had to
clean Mrs. Washington's classroom. We missed our ride with
Uncle Ollie. Didn't Queen tell you?"

Ma Pearl frowned down at me. "She pay you?"

I nodded and opened my hand to show her the three
quarters.

Her eyes bucked. "Whooweee! That heffa pay better'n Miz Robinson." She snatched the coins from my hand, then turned and stormed into the house without another word of correction.

Relieved to have that black strap out of my presence, I let out a puff of air.

Fred Lee approached me from behind and said, "I ain't go'n do that no mo'."

"Okay," I mumbled.

Even in the cool evening air, my brother was sweating. And I felt rotten about what I had done. I had lied to Uncle Ollie, my aunt Clara Jean's husband and Queen's stepdaddy, telling him we didn't need a ride home. I had lied to Mrs. Washington, though she detected it. I had lied to Ma Pearl, even though it wasn't the first time, and I knew it wouldn't it be the last. And I had risked my brother getting a beating just so I could meet up with Shorty Cooper and listen to him rant about killing white people. On top of all that, I didn't get to ask him a thing about my daddy.

I touched Fred Lee's arm. "I'm sorry."

He shrugged my hand away and stormed across the porch. "Jest don't do it no mo'," he said, opening the screen door. "You shouldn't be meetin' up with boys like that anyway. You might end up like Queen."

My jaw dropped. But before I could utter a word, Fred

Lee disappeared into the house, allowing the screen door to slam shut in my face.

End up like Queen? Tears sprang to my eyes. How could Fred Lee think something like that about me? I slumped down in one of the rickety chairs on the porch and allowed my book satchel to hit the floor with a thud. I would never sneak around with a boy like Queen had done. I cared too much about myself to get into that kind of trouble.

I didn't care that it would be dark in a few minutes and I would be left to sit alone in the night air. I didn't care that I hadn't eaten since noon—and then only a biscuit—and my stomach ached for food. Nor did I care that the sweet scent of Aunt Ruthie's cinnamon and sugar coated sweet potatoes floated from the kitchen to the porch. All I cared about was how my brother felt about me.

I picked up my history book from the porch and opened it in my lap. The white man's history is what Shorty had called it.

In seventh grade our teacher, Miss Johnson, had told us about a former slave named Frederick Douglass. She said that after Frederick Douglass escaped from slavery, he became a great speaker and even a writer. I couldn't imagine a colored man writing books during a time when colored people weren't allowed to learn how to read and write, but according to Miss Johnson, Frederick Douglass wrote three of them. She said that even folks back then found it hard to believe that he had once been a slave because they, like Mrs. Robinson's friends, thought colored people were incapable of learning.

I flipped through my history book and searched for information on Frederick Douglass. None could be found. As a matter of fact, Shorty was right. There was nothing in the book about colored people except that we had been enslaved by white folks.

I slammed the book shut, then flung it across the porch. And just as quickly as I had thrown it, I raced to the edge of the porch to retrieve it. "Don't disrespect nothing the white folks gives you," Papa always said. And I guess that included those raggedy textbooks they gave us for school.

Darkness set in quickly, and I knew I had to go inside the house. But little Abigail, Aunt Ruthie's one-year-old, had started her nightly screaming. And this time it was a suspected ear infection, seeing that she held her ear when she cried. The noise echoed from the living room and onto the porch.

If I hadn't written Aunt Belle that foolish letter, rather than sitting on that leaning porch, shivering in the November air, I could be in Saint Louis living in the fancy house she shared with Great-Aunt Isabelle. I could be a fancy city girl like Ophelia the Ogre, who came down to Mississippi with

Aunt Belle and Monty over the summer. I still remember the fancy pantsuit she wore, and I could still smell the sweetness of her perfume when I showed her the way to the toilet outside—even though she didn't actually have to use it! She only wanted to make fun of country people like me.

But that could have been me. I could have been like Ophelia the Ogre, if only I hadn't tried to be brave and decide to stay in Mississippi and claim my rights as a citizen. Now I was stuck in a war. A war I didn't ask for—a war I wasn't sure I knew how to fight.

After a moment of brooding, and after little Abigail quieted her screams, I finally gathered up my books and headed inside. Immediately upon entering the bedroom I shared with Queen, my left hand clenched into a fist.

Queen, who sat on her bed with Abigail bouncing on her knee, sneered at me and said, "Look what the cat drug in."

Though I wanted to take my fist and knock her into the middle of December, I was at least glad she knew how to quiet a fussy child. I squinted meanly at her and said, "Did you give Ma Pearl my message about cleaning up Mrs. Washington's classroom?"

Queen scowled. "What you think?"

"I think you didn't."

"Why should I lie for you?"

"Who said I was lying?"

Queen smirked. "I know a lie when I hear one."

"You should," I said, smirking right back at her. "Since you wouldn't know the truth if it came and bit you on the nose."

"You better watch yo'self, little girl. Wouldn't want them lies to come bite you on the butt."

"Like yours did?" I said, my brows raised.

"Don't worry 'bout me. I'm grown."

"You wanna be, but you ain't. Having a baby don't make you grown. It just means you're stupid."

Queen frowned and glared at me from head to toe. "Look who calling somebody stupid. You think I don't know you met that ol' black-as-night Shorty Cooper under a tree after school?"

My body felt like ice water had been tossed on it.

Before I bothered asking, she answered what I was thinking. "Ollie was late. But he showed up just in time." She smirked and said, "At least my baby won't be black as the ace of spades and dumber than a rock."

I felt like throwing up. I slumped down on the bed. "It wasn't like that," I murmured.

"Um-hmm," she said, sneering. "That's what they all say."

"I ain't having nobody's baby," I said, my teeth clenched. If it hadn't been for Abigail cooing in her lap, I would have pounced like a cat and clawed out Queen's eyes.

Queen fluttered her eyelids and sang, "Rose and Shorty sittin' in a tree. K-I-S-S-I—"

I didn't care that Abigail was on her knee, I hopped off my bed, lunged at Queen, and knocked her to the floor.

Both she and Abigail screamed so loud Ma Pearl came storming to our room.

Chapter Nine

WEDNESDAY, NOVEMBER 16

FIVE DAYS AFTER MY LEGS RECEIVED SEVEN LASHES from Ma Pearl's black strap of terror, they were still sore. And so was I. I was sore at Ma Pearl for not bothering to ask questions when she flew into the room swinging that strap with all her might, yelling at Queen and me that we were too old to be carrying on and making all that racket. Though she yelled at both of us, my legs were the only ones she aimed for with the discipline. Two lashes came immediately without any questions asked, then another five followed when Queen "explained" why we were arguing in the first place.

"She met a boy after school!" she cried, pointing at me.

When I tried to explain, even pointing out that Shorty was my cousin on my daddy's side, the force of the strap seemed to intensify. With each lash, Ma Pearl reminded me that I was not allowed to stay after school for any reason, especially not to meet a so-called cousin. Then, after sufficiently tanning *my* hide as she put it, she got Fred Lee, too, for having a part in my lie.

As I sat in church that Wednesday night, I tried to block all that out of my mind and listen to the lesson offered by Reverend Jenkins. He read from the book of Isaiah. It was a message about Jerusalem and the Jews, of course, but he compared it to the South and the Negroes.

And they shall build houses, and inhabit them. . . . They shall not build and another inhabit. "How many of y'all would love to have a house like the white man's whose place you live on?" Reverend Jenkins asked.

I wanted badly to raise my hand high and wave it like some of the others, but Ma Pearl was already glaring at me from the corner of her eye.

. . . and they shall plant vineyards, and eat the fruit of them. . . . they shall not plant, and another eat. Reverend Jenkins stared directly at Papa as he asked, "Brothers, wouldn't you like to sell that cotton you care for so tenderly every summer and put that money in a bank account for your own children's inheritance?"

Surprisingly, Papa nodded slightly. Ma Pearl rolled her eyes so hard at him that it's a wonder they didn't fall off her face. I didn't know if it was out of respect for Reverend Jenkins or if he really had a desire to have money in the bank like Mr. Robinson, but Papa's face brightened a bit at Reverend Jenkins's words. He always talked about being like the apostle Paul and content in whatever state he was in—whether he was poor or whether he was rich. I know I thought it was unfair that all the poor people worked the land while the landowner received all the profits. But did Papa?

. . . for as the days of a tree are the days of my people, and mine elect shall long enjoy the work of their hands. "The time is coming," Reverend Jenkins said, "when a Negro will no longer build a magnificent house just so another can reside there, the way our enslaved ancestors did. The time is coming," he said, "when God's elect shall enjoy the work of their own hands."

I didn't know where he was going with any of this, but I pictured the ancient oak in our front yard. It was twisted in every way imaginable, its long roots snaking almost to the house. That tree had to be older than Miss Addie, and she was nearly 102! In my mind, I couldn't imagine a day when a Negro in Mississippi wouldn't have to chop and pick cotton for a white man. But there was something in Reverend Jenkins's eyes that night. A fire. Not like the fire that Shorty wanted to set. But a spark that would shine brighter than a star. A spark that could change a people, a nation.

"The time is ripe for change," Reverend Jenkins said. "And we can't just sit around and allow the northern Negro to force that change. We've got to stand up for our own rights in the South."

He sounded like Shorty, whose words I couldn't get to leave my mind. I hadn't talked to him since Friday, because he hadn't been back to school. Even though field work kept him behind in school, the fact that for days he simply didn't show up probably contributed to his failure even more.

I knew he wanted to talk about a revolution, but I wanted to talk to him about my daddy, to see whether he knew anything about him. I myself knew very little. I had only seen him once, when I was barely two years old. And at thirteen, I, of course, couldn't remember what he looked like. Ma Pearl said I looked like him. But it's hard to know what you look like when you rarely get to see yourself in a mirror. Perhaps if Shorty knew my daddy, I could get to meet him somehow.

But for now, on this Wednesday night, I needed desperately to talk to Hallelujah, to share with him what Shorty had said. Since Sunday he had been avoiding me. I suspected that somehow word had gotten to him that I had met up with Shorty on Friday.

Each time I glanced at him, I caught him staring. Then he would quickly look away. I was sitting too far away from him to pass a note. My only option was to wait until the lesson was over and catch up with him at the fellowship table in the back, where platters of teacakes and hoop cheese and a couple of gallons of sweet tea awaited us.

Reverend Jenkins read a few more scriptures, then began

talking about how Moses led the Israelites out of Egypt and how, in the same way, Harriet Tubman had helped many slaves escape to freedom in the North.

"We don't need a Moses," he said. "Instead we need a Joshua. We need someone who will help us fight the giants in this land. We're not trying to escape. We are trying to conquer."

"Conquer" sounded too much like fighting to me. Real fighting. The kind Shorty was talking about. Surely a man as mild as Reverend Jenkins was not speaking of fighting.

As soon as the last word of the benediction had rolled off Reverend Jenkins's tongue, I was by Hallelujah's side — heading him off before he reached the fellowship table.

"Hey," I said, sidling up to him.

"Hey," he answered back. He barely looked my way.

My feelings were hurt, but I wasn't about to let him just saunter on over to that table and start talking to other people without saying another word to me. I yanked his arm and pulled him toward the door instead.

"Walk outside with me," I said.

Other young people had already stepped outside into the crisp night air. They loitered around the church and chatted about anything and everything except Reverend Jenkins's message. Normally, I would have done the same thing. But this time I not only wanted to know why Hallelujah seemed to be upset with me, but I also wanted to know about this fight Reverend Jenkins spoke of. Was it a figurative fight? Or a literal one?

"Would I be correct if I said you've been avoiding me?" I asked.

We stopped right at the bottom of the church steps and stood under the soft glow of the light on the tiny porch. Hallelujah, leaning on the porch post, crossed his arms over his chest and didn't answer me.

"Shorty's my cousin," I said, my voice strained.

Hallelujah gave me a sideways stare. "That's not what I'm worried about."

My forehead creased. "You're worried about me?"

Hallelujah dropped his hands to his sides and heaved a sigh. "Why would you have anything to do with a boy like Shorty? You heard the nonsense he was spewing out in Miss Hill's class. You know how bad he could make you look?"

"He *is* my cousin," I said. "I have a right to talk to my own cousin, don't I?"

"He's a troublemaker," Hallelujah said sharply.

"And just what were you doing Thursday morning when Miss Hill ran weeping out of the classroom?"

"Informing my peers," Hallelujah answered.

I couldn't argue with him, because information was certainly not what Shorty was interested in. He wanted a revolution. A fight. He wanted to kill white people. I shuddered at the thought.

"You shouldn't be seen with him," Hallelujah said. "Teachers don't think too highly of him."

I gave him a sideways glance. "From what I can tell, Miss Hill doesn't think too highly of you, either. But that doesn't stop me from being *your* friend. Besides, Shorty asked me to meet him after school. He said it was time for change and he needed my help. So I met him. What else was I supposed to do? And why the devil do you even care?"

Hallelujah gripped my shoulders as if to shake me. "Because you're my friend," he said.

"For the record, Shorty wanted to talk about the same thing your daddy was talking about tonight," I said. "He said it was time for change."

"It is. But not like he wants to."

"How do you know what he wants?"

Hallelujah mimicked Shorty. "'*You can march all you want, but I'm picking up my grandaddy's shotgun. I ain't go'n march on the street and git gunned out.*' I know what he wants. He wants the white man's blood running in the street instead of the colored man's feet marching in it."

"What about your daddy? And you? What do you want?"

"Change," Hallelujah answered briskly. "But it won't come by killing white people. It'll come by getting them to recognize that we're all equal. That one race isn't superior to another."

When he sat on the top step, I motioned for him to scoot over. I sat beside him. "Quit sounding so grown-up all the time."

He scoffed and said, "One of us has to."

I nudged him in the side. "I forgot. You're a man who's going places."

He grinned and nudged me back. "Yep. And I'm taking you with me."

"Where are we going, Hallelujah Jenkins?" I teased him.

He nodded and said, "Columbus, Ohio."

"For the man who discovered this great country," we both said together.

We laughed quietly for a moment, then Hallelujah's expression turned serious again. "Shorty sounds like Nat Turner."

Turner. Because the name sounded familiar, my first thought was that it was one of Ricky Turner's evil relatives. I scrunched up my face. I couldn't recall whether I'd heard of any of them with a name that sounded like an insect — gnat.

Noticing my puzzled expression, Hallelujah continued.

"He was a slave who thought he would one day be like Moses and lead his people to freedom."

"Oh," I said, nodding. "I remember hearing something about him."

"The only problem was, instead of letting the good Lord do the punishing the way he punished Pharaoh and the Egyptians when they wouldn't let his people go, Nat Turner took matters into his own hands. He led a slave revolt, taking a band of slaves with him from plantation to plantation, killing off white folks."

I shivered. "A revolt *does* sound like something Shorty would do. He said something about randomly killing a white person to show them what it feels like to be scared."

Hallelujah groaned. "The story goes that Nat Turner and his army killed about sixty white folks. But to bring down the rebellion, the authorities killed more than a hundred of Nat Turner's folks."

I swallowed. "Didn't they hang Nat Turner?"

Hallelujah nodded. "He got away for a minute. But they found him later and executed him."

Goose bumps covered my arms. "If Shorty tried something like that, he'd eventually be killed, just like Nat Turner."

"He's right about defending ourselves, but we can't go after people with guns on purpose."

"Is that why Reverend Jenkins said we need a Joshua and not a Moses?"

Hallelujah frowned. "Nat Turner was no Moses. He didn't lead any slaves to freedom. He led them to their deaths. Harriet Tubman was our Moses. She successfully led three hundred slaves to freedom without even one of them getting killed. And she didn't leave a bloody trail of white folks in her path either."

"Miss Johnson told us about her," I said. "But she never mentioned Nat Turner."

"Maybe she didn't want to give people like Shorty any ideas."

"So what did Reverend Jenkins mean about needing a Joshua, not a Moses?"

"I think he was referring to them marching around the walls of Jericho."

I nodded. "Like people are marching now."

We were silent for a moment before I asked what good marching would do.

"It's a start," said Hallelujah. "But we've got to do something more. Instead of marching, we need to stand."

I questioned him with raised brows.

"Stand up for our rights," said Hallelujah. "March right into some of these places where they say we can't go and stand there. Or sit. Or whatever it takes to make them see that we are people too."

I crossed my arms and said, "Oh, you mean like my cousin Mule, so we can get thrown in jail and beat up?"

Hallelujah shrugged. "If that's what it takes. Besides, I didn't say anything about punching someone in the face."

"Well, what are you gonna do when they ask you to leave?"

"Stay."

"What if they hit you?"

"Stay."

"You won't hit back?"

"No."

"You're crazy."

"I'm fed up."

"Like Mule, huh?"

"Well, yeah. But I won't hit anyone."

"This all sounds good—all this big talk about standing up for rights—but I think it's crazy to just go sit in a restaurant and demand to be served."

Hallelujah pointed at himself. "Then I'm crazy. And so is Dr. Howard, in Mound Bayou. He's holding meetings now. In churches. In large cities like New York. Encouraging people to take a stand. Especially for Emmett Till."

"Has he gone into any white restaurants and demanded to be served?"

The air went out of Hallelujah like a deflated balloon.

"You ever hear Dr. Howard give one of his speeches?" I asked, trying to make up for badgering him.

Hallelujah shook his head. "Not yet. But I sure would like to. Preacher's gotten word that his next speech might be in Montgomery, Alabama, soon."

Just the mention of Montgomery reminded me of Aunt Belle's fiancé, Monty, or Aaron Montgomery Ward Harris. He had stood up for me when Ma Pearl wanted me to quit school, and he had welcomed me to join him and Aunt Belle in Saint Louis. But I had chosen to stay because I thought I wanted to be a part of all this. This war, that might actually involve fighting.

"I would love to go hear Dr. Howard speak," Hallelujah said. "I wish more colored people could be like him. He's a surgeon, a farmer, a businessman, *and* a fighter for the rights of our people. Can you imagine what we could accomplish if more of our people believed in themselves the way he does?"

All I could do was sigh. I was *not* one of those people. I knew I was smart enough to go to college, but doubts once again had begun to creep up on me. I wanted so badly to be brave like Hallelujah. Like Reverend Jenkins. Like Dr. Howard. Even like Shorty, though I didn't want to kill anyone. And I had been brave once. I was brave back in September, while Aunt Belle and Monty were here. Perhaps their presence somehow gave me strength. But Reverend Jenkins had said that we had to find our own strength. That we shouldn't depend solely on the Negro from the North to save us. We had to save ourselves. Maybe I was depending too much on the North, or going north, rather. I had chosen to stay. I had chosen the South. I had made that clear in my letter to Aunt Belle. And she had applauded me in her return letter. "You are such a brave girl, Rosa Lee!" she had written.

When I laughed to myself and *at* myself, Hallelujah wrinkled his forehead and stared at me.

"Sorry," I said. "I was just thinking about something my aunt wrote me, and it made me laugh. She said I was brave."

"You are," Hallelujah replied.

I shook my head. "No. I'm scared."

Hallelujah put his hand on my shoulder. "You don't have to be."

"I don't want to die."

"You won't."

"How do you know?"

"Because I'll die trying to keep you alive."

Warmth spread over me. "Greater love hath no man than this," I said.

"That a man lay down his life for his friends," Hallelujah said.

"Friends again?" I asked.

Hallelujah smiled. "Forever."

When the church door creaked open and voices spilled out, we ended our conversation. Fellowship time was over. It was time to go home.

Chapter Ten

FRIDAY, NOVEMBER 18

When I saw Hallelujah that morning before school started, his smile seemed to stretch from one side of his face to the other. With Reverend Jenkins being a teacher, Hallelujah got to school before I did, and he was usually waiting for me outside the eighth grade classroom.

"What you so happy for this morning, besides the day being Friday?" I asked him.

"Guess where I might get to go."

With raised brows, I teased him. "Hunting?"

Hallelujah rolled his eyes. Many of the boys we knew went hunting during the winter months, and some of them even hunted with white boys. The most I could do was shake my head at any colored boy who was foolish enough to enter the woods with a white boy carrying a loaded shotgun.

"So, where might you get to go?" I asked him.

Hallelujah's eyes shone brighter, and his grin stretched broader. "Alabama."

Both my eyebrows shot up. "Montgomery? You're going to hear Dr. Howard speak?"

"Well, it's not confirmed. But Preacher's almost certain Montgomery will be his next stop. Next Sunday, right after Thanksgiving. And if it is, he says we can go."

I groaned and said, "I'm jealous." But I couldn't contain my smile.

"Jealous people don't smile," said Hallelujah.

"Okay, then. I'm happy *and* I'm jealous. Wish I could do stuff like that."

I was surprised to see Hallelujah's smile fade. It was no secret to him that I had never set foot outside Stillwater. I had never even been to Greenwood, though my own mama had once lived there. I could tell he felt sorry for me.

"I wish you could go too," he said.

I playfully punched his arm and said, "This will be something you can tell your grandchildren one day."

"Yeah," Hallelujah said, his tone sarcastic. "I can tell them I had to go halfway across the state of Mississippi and travel down the whole state of Alabama, just to hear a man from my own backyard make a speech."

"Well, when you put it that way, it does sound kind of crazy. Why all the way in Alabama? Why not here, in Mississippi?"

"There's a young preacher there, named Martin Luther King. He invited Dr. Howard to speak at his church. Dexter Avenue Baptist Church. It's the church where a lot of the NAACP folks in Montgomery attend."

I smiled and said, "And you, Hallelujah Jenkins, will be right there among them."

Hallelujah beamed. "Yep. Hearing Dr. Howard speak will be a dream come true. I've been wanting to go to one of his rallies ever since that racist jury declared Roy Bryant and J. W. Milam not guilty."

I groaned again. "Don't remind me," I said, even though that trial was always fresh in my mind.

As students streamed into the building, Hallelujah and I said our goodbyes; he headed toward the ninth grade homeroom while I entered Miss Hill's class.

Shorty hadn't been to school the whole week. But that Friday there he was, sitting in his seat by the window, staring out.

Miss Hill, who had worn a smile all week, now wore a frown.

Since class hadn't started, I seized the opportunity to have a word with Shorty. When I reached his desk, the reek of his cigarettes caught me off guard and made me gag. Without thinking, I covered my nose with my sleeve. And just as I did,

Shorty looked toward me. If he was offended by my action, he didn't let it show. "Hey," he said.

"Where you been all week?" I asked.

He shrugged, then began picking at his nails. "Takin' care o' bizness."

"What kind of business?"

"Personal." He grinned and said, "Don't worry. It ain't got nothin' to do with killin' white folks, if that's what you wond'rin' 'bout."

"You working?" I asked.

Shorty shook his head. "Nah. Ain't no work for a field hand this time o' year."

"Then what you been doing all week?" I asked, my forehead creased.

Shorty chuckled. "You sho' is nosy this moan'n, ain't you?"

Seeing that he wasn't going to tell me why he hadn't been in school, I jumped straight to the real reason I wanted to talk to him. "Are we cousins?" I asked.

"Yo' daddy and my daddy brothers." Shorty smiled and rubbed his chin. "Don't I look like a Banks?"

"I don't know," I said, shrugging. "Other than my brother and me, I've never seen any of the Bankses."

"You—" Shorty cocked his head. "You ain't never see'd none o' yo' folks?"

I shook my head. "Nope."

"I'on see my daddy much, but I see yo' daddy all the time."

"Really?"

Shorty nodded.

"My—" I had a million questions. But before I could ask one, Miss Hill ordered us all to our seats.

"Maybe I'll ketch up with you in the lunchroom," Shorty suggested.

I nodded. It was all I could do to keep from shouting.

I barely heard a word any teacher said before lunchtime. My mind was on nothing except talking to Shorty about my daddy. All this time I had pretended I didn't care that he wasn't involved in my life. But truthfully, every time I saw Mr. Pete with Sugar and Lil' Man, I wanted a daddy in my life too. I knew it was too late to have that kind of relationship, and I had sense enough not to expect it, seeing I was already thirteen. But it would be nice during my teenage years if I could have a daddy to talk to sometimes, the way Hallelujah had Reverend Jenkins.

Seven minutes after I sat at my usual table in the back corner of the lunchroom, Shorty still hadn't shown up. I normally saved a spot for Hallelujah, who would come in fifteen minutes after us, with the ninth-graders. I was hoping to have gleaned all the information I needed from Shorty before then.

Instead of eating, I glanced back and forth between the doorway and the clock on the lunchroom wall, hoping Shorty would appear soon. Finally he did. But only after nine whole minutes had passed.

He strolled over and dropped down onto the bench next to me.

"Where were you?" I demanded.

He patted his shirt pocket. "Smoke."

I figured as much when the stench reached my nose. "It takes that long to smoke a cigarette?"

"I smoked two." Shorty clasped his long fingers together and placed his hands before him on the table. His hands were callused and ashy. If nothing else, they indicated he was a hard worker. Noticing me staring at his hands, he stared at them too. He held up his right hand, turning it back and forth, observing it as if for the first time. "That cotton field sho' is rough, ain't it?"

I glanced at my own rough hands and nodded.

"So, what was you 'bout to say in Hill's room this moan'n?

My daddy ever ask about me? That's what I wanted to ask Shorty. Instead, I found myself asking, "What's he like?"

Shorty shrugged. "He a good man."

"What's makes him good?"

"He help a lotta peoples."

He a good man. He help a lotta peoples. I had to let those words sink in. That wasn't the picture I had of my daddy. He had never done anything for me and Fred Lee. He had never bothered coming out to Mr. Robinson's place to see us except that one time he came to see whether Fred Lee looked like him — as if *that* was the most important thing in the world.

"Who does he help?" I asked. I felt an edge coming into my voice. I didn't want to appear angry. But the thought of my daddy helping other people while having done nothing for my brother and me made something dark rise in me.

"He help me, for one," said Shorty. "And Papa Ray and Mama Vee. We cain't make it on what we makes in the field."

A grunt slipped out of me.

Shorty shook his head. "I'on know what we'd do without Johnny Lee. He bought me that truck." He nodded toward the lunchroom window.

Shorty's truck was such a piece of junk that it was obvious Johnny Lee couldn't have bought it when it was new. Otherwise, that would mean he'd bought it for Shorty when he was a baby. But whether he bought it new or as the bucket of bolts that it was now, I was still upset. Papa always said that a man who won't take care of his own family is worse than an infidel.

I thought about Mama marrying Mr. Pete, taking care of his children, leaving for Chicago for a better life for them, promising to send money to Ma Pearl to help out with me and Fred Lee. But four months after she left, we'd only heard from her once. And the promised money was not included in the letter.

Whatever an infidel was, Mama was one too.

"Johnny Lee don't never come see y'all?" Shorty asked.

I shook my head. "Nope."

Shorty looked perplexed. "That ain't like Johnny Lee," he said.

I shrugged and said, "He came out to Mr. Robinson's place once. Fred Lee was a baby. I wasn't even two. I don't remember anything but my mama telling him to leave before my grandma caught him."

Shorty seemed to shiver. "I heard 'bout yo' granmama. Heard she ain't one to cross."

"You think that might be why Johnny Lee doesn't come see us?"

Shorty shook his head. "I'on know. But I know he a good man."

This time I didn't stifle my grunt.

"So you ain't never see'd Willow 'n 'em then?"

"Who is *Willow?*"

"Yo' lil' susta." Shorty leaned back and squinted at me. "She look jest like you."

"Her name is *Willow?* Like a tree?"

Shorty laughed. "You named afta a flower. What's the

difference?" He held up three fingers and rattled off Johnny Lee's children. "Betty Jean. Willow Mae. Johnny Junior."

"How old are they?"

"Betty Jean seven. Willow Mae nine. Johnny Junior 'leven."

"My brother's only twelve. Johnny Lee didn't waste any time starting his new family after checking to see if Fred Lee looked like him."

"No sense bein' bitter 'bout it. We all got problems. My daddy and Johnny Lee brothers, but my daddy don't have nothin' to do with me." Shorty shrugged. "I guess Johnny Lee takin' up the slack."

"Well, me and Fred Lee don't have *your* daddy taking up the slack for Johnny Lee. We've had to grow up without a mama and a daddy."

Shorty stared hard at me. "You got Preacha' Jenkins."

"Not the same," I said, shrugging. "He's the preacher. He has to take up time with his church members."

Shorty shook his head. "Nah, he don't. Girl, you blessed that peoples like them Jenkinses take up time wit'choo. Be grateful."

I ignored his admonition to be grateful and asked, "You think you might see Johnny Lee before next week?"

"I should."

"Since it's Thanksgiving, maybe he can come see me and

Fred Lee. My grandma probably wouldn't mind since it's a holiday. She's usually nice on holidays."

Shorty nodded. "I'a let him know."

"Thanks. I appreciate it."

Shorty smiled. "Ain't no trouble."

I pulled my biscuits from my lunch sack, unwrapped them, and offered him one.

He shook his head. "I eats a big breakfast. Don't need no midday meal."

I took a bite of one of my biscuits and chewed heartily. I didn't eat a big breakfast. I looked forward to my midday meal even if it consisted only of a couple of biscuits and, occasionally, a piece of fried salt pork.

"Now that I helped you," Shorty said, "maybe you can help me."

Just as he said that, the ninth-graders entered the lunchroom.

Shorty glanced toward the door. "Guess I need to git outta y'all's way."

Guilt grabbed me. I knew Hallelujah would not be happy that Shorty was sitting in his spot, nor would he join us at the table. But how could I just ask Shorty to leave after he'd been so kind to me?

I shook my head. "It's okay. Hallelujah will understand. I mean, we're first cousins, right?"

"He thank I'm ign'ant, don't he?"

I didn't answer. I finished up my second biscuit and took a quick glance toward Hallelujah. He stared back at me, then strolled away and joined some ninth-graders at another table.

"Well, I ain't," Shorty said. "I might not have book smarts like y'all, but I know 'bout life. And I know that if we don't fight, these white folks go'n keep killin' us. They ain't go'n care who they shoot. They kil't a fo'teen-year-old boy jest for whistlin' at a white woman. Beat him near death. Shot him in the head. Tied a cotton gin fan 'round his neck. Thowed him in the Tallahatchie River. These peckerwoods'a do anything to a Negro."

My forehead creased. "What's that got to do with Hallelujah?"

Shorty side-glanced at Hallelujah and muttered, "Nothin'. Jest takin' out my frustrations on the wrong folks, I reckon."

I reminded him why he was still at the table rather than Hallelujah. "What do you need me to do for you?"

Shorty studied me for a moment, then frowned. "You ain't the right person."

"The right person for what?"

"This ain't somethin' you'a do, so I ought not to tell you 'bout it."

"How do you know what I'll do unless you ask?"

With his forehead creased, Shorty sized me up. "A girl like you won't have the guts."

I straightened my shoulders and said, "Try me."

"Yo' grandaddy got a shotgun?"

"Of course."

"He usin' it?"

I shrugged. "He's never had to."

Shorty smiled. "That's what I figured." With his head tilted to the side, he asked, "You thank he'll let me use it?"

"Why do you need to use my granddaddy's shotgun?"

"Don't wor' 'bout it," Shorty said, shaking his head. "You ain't the right person to be talkin' 'bout this with. You too young and innocent."

"This is the second time you've asked for my help, and again you won't tell me what you want."

Shorty nodded in Hallelujah's direction. "First I thought I needed the lil' preacha'," he said. "But he like you. He too holy for this."

"You still talking about fighting?"

Shorty shook his head. "Nah. Not no mo'. I been talkin' with some fellas, and we come up with another plan. We'on need to fight. We jest need to put some fear in these white folks like they been doin' to us."

"Why'd you ask me about a shotgun?"

"We needs some. Right now we got two. Needs two mo'."

"We who?" I asked.

"Jest me and a few other fellas that's fed up with these white folks gunnin' down Negroes."

"What y'all planning on doing?"

Shorty frowned. "Go'n shoot out a few windas."

"Car windows?"

Shorty shook his head. "Nah. House windas."

"*House* windows? Whose house?"

Shorty leaned toward me and whispered, "Some o' these crackers'."

I squinted at him. "You're gonna shoot at white folks' houses?"

Shorty leaned back and crossed his arms. "I knowed a girl like you wouldn't have the guts to help us out."

"No," I said, "I don't have the guts. But I got good sense. And you should have more sense than that. How you gonna get away with shooting out white folks' windows without going to jail? Or worse, getting yourself killed?"

Shorty scoffed. "The same way white folks been doin' it for years. We go'n do it at night. They call theyselves night riders, right? Well, we go'n be the *black knight* riders."

I leaned in and hissed at him, "That's crazy!"

"We ain't go'n shoot nobody," Shorty said, now whispering so low that I could barely hear him. "Jest scare 'em."

"How many *fellas* you talking about?"

"Me and maybe six mo'. I still gotta round 'em up. But we go'n need mo' shotguns. I ain't got but one. And another fella got one."

I shook my head. "Well, you ain't gettin' Papa's."

"I knowed I should'na asted you." He nodded toward Hallelujah. "Now you go'n run 'n tell Jenkins, ain't you?"

I ignored his question. "What if you actually hit somebody while you're trying to do this so-called scaring?"

"Look. We ain't go'n hit nobody, a'right? It'a be in the middle o' the night. We jest go'n drive by, shoot out some windas of a few white folks' houses. Let 'em know they needs to be on the lookout too. Let 'em know we armed 'n dangerous jest like they is."

"Good Lord." I exhaled. "What if somebody's sitting by the window? You ever consider that, Shorty Cooper?"

"Ain't our problem if they decides to stay up late."

I waved my hands in frustration. "You and whoever your *fellas* happen to be can't just go out in the middle of the night and shoot at white folks' houses. For one, you might kill somebody. And two, it just ain't right."

"They killin' us, and they 'on even care." He drew in his breath and grew quiet for a moment.

After shifting his eyes around the room, he said, "You know there way mo' of us than there is o' them?"

I nodded. "Um-hmm. That's what my aunt told my grandma after Emmett Till was kidnapped. She said we should stand up to white people, since we outnumber them. But you see what happened at that trial. It ain't just the number of the people who matter, but the power they have."

"It's time we take away some o' that power," Shorty said. "And we start by showin' them what it feel like to live in fear."

"You ever stepped in an ant pile?"

Shorty's eyebrows shot up. "Ant pile? What that got to do with anything?"

"Have you?"

Shorty cut his eyes at me. "Yeah. One time."

"All of them rush up your foot and bite like crazy, don't they?"

"Girl, what is you gittin' at?"

"There are more of them than there are of you, but in the end, you still manage to get them all off your foot and destroy them."

"I ain't go'n jest stand there and let no lil' bitty ants eat up my foot. I'm bigger than they is. I'm go'n kill 'em."

"Well, think about that before you and your *black knights* go out and shoot at white folks' houses," I said. "They have the law on their side, and the law is bigger than you and your fellas."

I glanced toward Hallelujah. I caught him staring at me,

but he quickly turned away. I sighed and faced Shorty. "You ever hear of Nat Turner?"

"Yeah, I know who Nat Turner was," he said. "He was a fighter. He had a vision. His mama told him when he was a boy that he was go'n deliver his peoples. Just like Moses."

"You know he got killed by the law, right?"

Shorty squinted at me. "I done told ya, we ain't 'bout to bust up in no white folks' house 'n shoot 'em like Nat did. We ain't go'n do no mo' to them than them night riders be doin' to us. What you thank the white man did afta Abraham Lincoln freed the slaves?

"They went afta the folks that left. Kil't 'em. Prob'ly didn't thank twice 'bout it either. Right afta the war, bunch a whites kil't off colored soldiers, plus womens and chi'ren, right up there in Memphis. Ast Jenkins 'bout it. I'm sho' he know 'bout that riot up in Memphis. Happened in 1866."

"You sure know a lot for somebody who—"

"Don't go to school that much?" Shorty asked, his brows raised. "Jest 'cause I don't study the white man's history don't mean I don't know my own. The white man Mama Vee used to work for had a whole bunch a papers and notes on Negro history. Mama Vee used to sneak 'em to me and let me read 'em."

I narrowed my eyes at Shorty. "You really planning on shooting at white folks' houses?"

"They doin' worse than that to us."

"Nobody's shooting at you."

"Not yet."

"Why would a white person wanna kill you? You haven't done anything. You ain't NAACP, or out trying to get colored people registered to vote."

Shorty grimaced. "You thank that's the only reason they'a shoot a Negro? Did that Chicago boy do somethin' worthy o' death? Was he NAACP? Was he roundin' up Negroes takin' 'em to the coathouse?

"Nah, he wadn't doin' none o' that. And even if he did whistle at that lil' white woman, it wadn't no reason for him to git beat half to death. So don't try to tell me that white folks gotta have a reason to shoot a Negro. We ain't gotta do nothin' but look at 'em wrong."

I thought about how Mrs. Robinson had scolded me for having the audacity to smile back at Mrs. Jamison. She made it sound as if I had committed a crime.

Yet there was Mrs. Jamison, in that room full of women who wanted to keep the races separate—she had not only smiled at me, but she had also spoken out against the injustice of segregation.

"Not all white people are bad," I said to Shorty. "Not all of them want to kill colored people for voting or being a part of the NAACP."

"I know all 'em ain't bad," Shorty said. "The man Mama Vee used to work for wadn't too bad hisself. But I wouldn't say he was good either. Git him 'round the wrong white folks and he mighta turn't on her."

I didn't think Mrs. Jamison would do that. She had stood her ground with those ladies. "Well, if you're crazy enough to shoot at white folks' houses, don't shoot at the Jamisons' house. They at least try to be nice to colored people."

Shorty winced. "I'a do my best. But in the dark, everybody's house jest might look the same."

Chapter Eleven

WEDNESDAY, NOVEMBER 23

I WAS SICK FOR TWO DAYS AFTER TALKING WITH Shorty. Thoughts of him and other colored boys sneaking around Stillwater in the middle of the night, shooting at the windows of white folks' houses, spun around in my head like a whirlwind. By the end of the day the whirling had attacked my stomach. I was so sick that I couldn't eat supper.

What if Shorty carried out his plans, and white folks retaliated? It could be like that riot he talked about that happened in Memphis. Stillwater could turn into a bloody battleground.

I had never believed in fasting before. But that weekend I fasted involuntarily. Hardly a crust of bread passed my lips. All I wanted to do was lie in my bed and pray.

When I returned to school on Monday, Shorty wasn't there, and Hallelujah wouldn't talk to me. He didn't say a word to me on Tuesday or Wednesday either. Which is why I was surprised when he passed me a note in church on Wednesday night.

"Why were you sitting with him?" the note read.

I cut my eyes at him before I lowered my head and scribbled, "When your daddy gave us paper and pencil for note taking, I don't think this is what he had in mind."

Hallelujah scoffed at my note. "You've done it before," he wrote back.

"So?" I mouthed.

"What did he want?" Hallelujah mouthed back.

I wrote: "We talked about my daddy."

Hallelujah's face twisted in puzzlement. I gestured for him to return the note to me.

"My daddy might come see us tomorrow. For Thanksgiving," I wrote.

When Hallelujah read the note, a smile spread across his face. I smiled too—happy at the prospect of my daddy coming to see me. But then I glanced at Ma Pearl a few pews ahead of me and wondered whether she'd even allow him in the house. I decided to offer up a quick prayer that she would. With all the darkness swirling around me, I needed something good to happen in my life.

Hoping I had satisfied Hallelujah, I turned my attention back to Reverend Jenkins. But I should have known Hallelujah wouldn't let the conversation drop there. He passed me another note.

"So, what else did you talk about?" the note read.

I didn't want to tell Hallelujah about my conversation

with Shorty, especially since Shorty had predicted I'd "run 'n tell Jenkins." I had to think of something quickly.

But the next words out of Reverend Jenkins's mouth sent chills up my arms. "Wherefore putting away lying," he said, "speak every man truth with his neighbor."

My eyes quickly turned to the podium. *Why do you always do this to me?* I wanted to scream.

"Good people have been lying for centuries," Reverend Jenkins said. "Abraham did it. His son Isaac did it. Isaac's son Jacob did it. Even King David, the man after God's own heart, did it. But the apostle Paul said in his letter to the Ephesians to put away lying, and speak truth with your neighbor."

What difference would it make if I told Hallelujah about Shorty's plans? Would he tell Reverend Jenkins? Would Reverend Jenkins have a talk with Shorty and try to stop him? Would Shorty be mad at me and not help me connect with my daddy?

But what if Shorty was right? What if white folks would change if they knew how it felt to be terrorized for no reason?

I thought about that day Ricky Turner threatened me on the road. One of his buddies had hurled a tobacco-spit-filled beer bottle at my head. Then Ricky shouted, "Next time it'll be a bullet, you coon!" He did this for no other reason than to instill fear of himself in me.

When Hallelujah faked a cough, I glanced his way.

Pretending to scribble, he motioned for me to answer his question.

Speak every man truth with his neighbor. Well, technically, I wasn't a man, and Hallelujah wasn't my neighbor. So I wrote, "Nothing. Just talked about my daddy and my half-sisters and brother."

Hallelujah read my note with a smile that seemed to say, "Oh, that's nice." Then he scribbled something back. "The looks on your faces made me think it was something more serious."

I glanced over at Hallelujah.

He frowned.

He knew I was lying.

Guilt punched me in the gut. But the pain it left didn't outweigh the shame of wondering whether Shorty was right. Or Hallelujah was wrong.

I wrote, "Shorty said something about a riot in Memphis. In 1866?"

Lines crossed Hallelujah's forehead as he read. He frowned and began his note on a fresh piece of paper. From a glance, it seemed his words would occupy most of the paper.

Hallelujah's note read: "Started with white policemen and Negro soldiers. Ended with lynch mobs of whites killing Negro men, women, and children. Negro homes robbed. Negro churches and schools burned. Terrible tragedy."

I wrote, "Sounds a little like the Nat Turner tragedy."

Hallelujah raised his eyebrows when he read the note. "Don't get any crazy ideas," he wrote back.

I shook my head and mouthed, "I won't."

He beckoned for the note, then scribbled, "And Shorty?"

I hesitated but shook my head.

Hallelujah shot me a doubtful look.

I scribbled on the note: "That's all we talked about. I swear. Now stop passing notes."

Hallelujah read the note, sighed, then tucked it inside his Bible.

I released a breath and relaxed my knotted-up shoulders. Luckily, with it being the night before Thanksgiving, there would be no fellowship after Bible study. Folks wanted to get home and prepare their meals for the holiday.

I wouldn't have to talk to Hallelujah. It was one thing to write a lie. It's was a whole nother thing to have to speak one.

Chapter Twelve

THURSDAY, NOVEMBER 24

AFTER NEARLY A WEEK HAD PASSED AND I HAD HEARD nothing about a band of Negro youth terrorizing white people in the middle of the night, I fixed my thoughts on enjoying one of the two days each year that Ma Pearl seemed to act halfway decently toward her fellow human beings — Thanksgiving and Christmas.

I was nine years old the first time I remember celebrating Thanksgiving. It was something Ma Pearl wanted to do because the Robinsons did it. And from what I'd heard, the Robinsons began doing it because the president of the United States declared that the fourth Thursday of November would be a national day of thanks. Papa said it was a shame that the president had to remind people to give thanks when the good Lord has been trying to tell us that all along.

We gathered around the kitchen table right at noon. For once we didn't have to eat one of our own chickens. Mr. Robinson sent Ma Pearl home with a plump turkey and a store-bought ham. I'd been wanting one of those hams since the day I humiliated myself by eating the leftover sandwiches of the Cackling Church Club.

Our table was piled with food—turkey, ham, dressing, collard greens, yams, smashed potatoes, creamed corn, field peas, cornbread, and butter rolls. In the gleaming white safe awaited the cakes—caramel, coconut, lemon, and chocolate—and pies—pecan and sweet potato. The eyes of Aunt Ruthie's poor children seemed as if they would pop right out of their heads if they didn't eat soon.

But before we could eat, there would be the scripture reading and prayer. Each person was expected to memorize a scripture regarding thanksgiving and say it before we ate. Papa started us off by quoting from heart Colossians 3:15: *And let the peace of God rule in your hearts, to the which also ye are called in one body; and be ye thankful.*

One by one, my family quoted memorized scripture on thanksgiving. Ma Pearl: *Give thanks to the Lord for he is good.* Aunt Ruthie: *In everything give thanks.* Queen: *Give thanks always.*

When it was my turn, something snapped in me and my mind went blank. I couldn't remember the scripture I had memorized the night before. The only one stuck in my head was the one Papa had quoted: *Let the peace of God rule in your hearts.*

With all the Negro blood that had been shed in Mississippi in the last few months, how could Papa talk about peace ruling in our hearts? My mind began to race—not in search of scripture but in search of some kind of sense to everything that was going on around me. My grandfather was speaking of peace. My best friend was speaking of peaceful protests. And my cousin was speaking of retaliation. *Fear for fear.* What if that plan to instill fear grew into something more? What if it grew into a fight? *Bloodshed for bloodshed.*

"Gal, is you go'n say somethin'?" Ma Pearl interrupted my thoughts.

"Umm. J-Jesus wept," I stammered.

Ma Pearl furrowed her brows. "Jesus wept? That ain't no Thanksgiving strip'chur."

Papa, too, frowned at me. "Now, Rose. I know you can do better than that."

My throat went dry. No, Papa, I can't do better than that. I can't be like you no matter how hard I try. I can't let peace rule in my heart when my heart is constantly broken by my circumstances. Yes, I probably should have been thankful seeing we had a table full of food before us. I knew a lot of people who would have given anything to have a feast like the one Mr. Robinson made sure we had. There was much to be thankful for. But sadly, there was even more to be bitter about.

Little Abigail had begun to fidget in Aunt Ruthie's arms, and I knew I was holding up the dinner. I knew I had to quote a scripture and move on. But my brain seemed as smashed as those creamy white potatoes. *Jesus wept. Jesus wept. Jesus wept.*

Suddenly, a scripture popped into my head. And before I had time to consider the consequence, it had spilled from my mouth. "I didn't come to bring peace but a sword."

I quickly covered my mouth with both of my hands.

"Gal, what the devil is wrong wit'choo!" Ma Pearl cried.

With my hands still cupped over my mouth, all I could do was shake my head. This wasn't what I wanted to say. I wanted to give thanks like everyone else. I wanted to pretend we lived in a good place, that we were as happy as the Robinsons were in their big white house, sitting around their fine oak table, in their wallpapered dining room, enjoying the fruit of their Negro laborers.

But I couldn't pretend. My stomach knotted at the thought of the Robinsons and the fact that they were free. They could go to town and shop in any store without having to stand around and wait until all the white customers were served. They could eat anywhere they wanted without having to check for signs to see whether their kind was served there. They could drink water from a fountain where the water was actually cold and didn't taste as metallic as an iron pipe. Nor did they have to cast their eyes downward when approached by the opposite race. And even though Papa was nearly twenty years older than Mr. Robinson, it was Papa who addressed him as "sir" and not the other way around.

A frown overtook my face, but I somehow managed to utter, "And when ye will offer a sacrifice of thanksgiving unto the Lord, offer it at your own will." Before the words finished crossing my lips, I knew they were just as wrong as the peace and sword scripture.

I braced myself for a slap.

But Thanksgiving truly was a good day for Ma Pearl. Instead of slapping me across the room, she smiled and nodded at Fred Lee. "Go on, chile" she said.

Fred Lee's voice shook when he spoke. "Let us come before his presence with thanksgiving."

Ma Pearl nodded again, then addressed Aunt Ruthie. "Any yo' young'uns got a strip'chur?"

"Yes'sum," Aunt Ruthie muttered. Her voice, too, shook. It seemed I had shaken up the whole family with my foolish tongue.

Lil' John, Virgil, Mary Lee, and even two-year-old Alice quoted a scripture. I thought Ma Pearl would smile. Instead she seemed disappointed that Aunt Ruthie had trained her children well. Or perhaps she was upset that I had fumbled like a fool while children younger than six quoted scriptures without a quiver.

The food and the conversation were lively. Even Aunt Ruthie, for once, was happy. Queen, with baby Abigail now bouncing on her knee, wasn't allowing her predicament to spoil her day of thanks either. But I could not involve myself in the merriment. That whole business about peace wouldn't leave my mind. There I was, my thoughts dark, wondering why I was sitting among these people who were so content with their sad way of life that they could enjoy a token turkey from the man who was barely better than a slave master toward them. And poor Queen! That man, Mr. Robinson, would even be the never-acknowledged grandfather of the child she was carrying. How *could* she smile?

A knock at the front door startled me.

Johnny Lee. Shorty had come through for me.

My body stiffened. What would Ma Pearl think? What would she *do*?

Even though I was not even two years old when it

happened, I still remember the day he came to the house to see Fred Lee when he was a baby. I can still hear the panic in Mama's voice when she said, "You need to leave 'fo my mama catch you here."

I noticed Aunt Ruthie seemed to stiffen too. Perhaps she thought it was her mean-as-the-devil husband, Slow John, at the door.

I jumped up to rush to the front door before Papa could move his chair from the table.

Ma Pearl glared at me. "Gal, what is you doin'? Set yo'self down 'fo I knock you back down. Didn't nobody ast you to git the do'."

When I plopped back down on my chair, even Fred Lee eyed me suspiciously.

Papa took his time pushing his chair from the table and getting up. "Prob'ly Clara Jean and Ollie," he said, referring to Queen's mama and stepdaddy.

Ma Pearl sucked her teeth. "Long as it ain't Slow John. 'Cause he ain't gittin' a lick o' food from *this* table."

Jesus, I prayed, *if it's Johnny Lee, please let Ma Pearl offer him a lick of food rather than a lick from her mighty fist.*

My anticipation was short-lived. I let out a sigh when I heard the voices of Hallelujah and Reverend Jenkins once

Papa answered the door. But the day wasn't over. Perhaps my daddy would still come.

I was surprised to see Hallelujah's aunt Bertha trailing behind them when they came back to the kitchen. Her visits to our house were almost as rare as that Thanksgiving turkey sent over by Mr. Robinson. That's because Ma Pearl was not one of Miss Bertha's favorite people.

Educated at the colored college, Tougaloo, like her brother, Reverend Jenkins, Miss Bertha Jenkins was one of those Negroes who could have easily chosen the North over the South. And she could have just as easily chosen a bigger place to live, such as Greenwood, rather than lowly Stillwater. Yet there she was, just like a few other educated Negroes, trying to make life fairer, as she said, for those who couldn't leave. She operated a small store in town, and her store, unfortunately, had been vandalized numerous times in an attempt to get her to close it down. Nothing was ever done about the break-ins, which were dismissed—much like the Emmett Till case—as Negroes destroying their own property and blaming God-fearing whites in an attempt to make them look bad.

"Y'all c'mon in," Ma Pearl called to the trio standing near the doorway. "Y'all chi'ren git up and make room," she ordered us. Fred Lee and I gave our seats to Reverend Jenkins and Miss Bertha, while Queen, rather than give up her seat for Hallelujah, stayed put.

Miss Bertha might not have cared much for Ma Pearl, but she loved me like a little sister. I was the first person in the kitchen whom she came to and embraced. And unlike nearly everyone else who had known me most of my life, she called me by my new name, Rosa, rather than Rose. She was also tall, and movie-star beautiful, like Mama.

With the Jenkins family cramped along with us in our kitchen, I no longer felt alone. I no longer felt like the only one who could not be happy with the way things were in our state.

Hallelujah sat on the bench next to the window, and I joined him there. Fred Lee, as he did often, slipped out of the kitchen unnoticed and escaped to the back porch. I was surprised that Aunt Ruthie's two boys, Lil' John and Virgil, didn't follow him, as they had become his unofficial second and third shadows.

I was still nervous that Hallelujah would bring up the issue with Shorty, but I leaned over anyway and whispered, "Glad y'all came." Because I was.

Hallelujah reassured me with a smile and said, "Preacher has a surprise for you."

My heart fluttered. A surprise? Reverend Jenkins was

known to stop by on Christmas and surprise Queen, Fred Lee, and me with small gifts. But this was Thanksgiving, so I couldn't help wonder what kind of surprise awaited me.

"For all of us?" I asked Hallelujah.

He shook his head. "Just you."

My heart pounded with anticipation. I had already received a Bible, so that certainly, thank goodness, wasn't the surprise. A book, perhaps? Maybe Reverend Jenkins had changed his mind about allowing me to read the book *Native Son*, which was written by a colored man named Richard Wright, who was born in Mississippi. Hallelujah had promised to bring it by for me to read it back in September when Ma Pearl wouldn't allow me to attend school, but Hallelujah said Reverend Jenkins claimed the book wasn't proper reading for a lady—which I assured him I was not.

"Is it the book, *Native Son*?" I asked Hallelujah.

With a bewildered look, he frowned and shook his head. "No. This is better than a book."

My fingers tingled. Not a Bible. Not a book. But a surprise. When I heard my name mentioned, I leaned in toward the table to catch a whiff of the conversation. Hallelujah sat on the edge of the bench. His right foot tapped anxiously against the wood floor. And his smile was brighter than a midday sun.

But when Ma Pearl yelled out, "Nah, she cain't go," Hallelujah's smile faded quicker than a September sunset.

"But Miss Sweet," said Reverend Jenkins, "when I asked you this last night, you said you would give it serious consideration."

"And I did," Ma Pearl answered briskly. "I thought about it. I thought for sho' I was go'n let her go. Woulda been good for her to git outta here for once." She shook her head. "But after today, I don't know what to thank o' Rose. That gal ack like she done lost her mind. Couldn't even say a decent strip'chur for Thanksgiving."

I shot Hallelujah a confused look.

He mouthed, "Alabama."

"Montgomery?" I mouthed back.

Hallelujah nodded.

I pointed at myself.

Hallelujah nodded again and whispered, "Yes, you. Preacher wants to take you to Montgomery with us Saturday."

My mouth fell open. That's why Ma Pearl was so calm after I got smart-mouthed with her. She wanted to hold it against me later. She knew all along that Reverend Jenkins was coming over to ask for permission for me to go to Alabama with them. It pleased her to have a reason to say no. She sat there and talked so badly about me that it was as if I wasn't even in the room.

Though the kitchen was crowded, I knew we couldn't talk there. I had to find an excuse to get outside, or to slip out unnoticed, like Fred Lee.

"Aunt Ruthie," I whispered. "Want me to take the children outside?"

Aunt Ruthie smiled her consent. She always knew exactly what I needed.

Chapter Thirteen

THURSDAY, NOVEMBER 24

So, y'all really are going to hear Dr. Howard speak?" I asked Hallelujah once we got Aunt Ruthie's children off the porch and playing in the front yard.

"Yeah," Hallelujah answered with a nod. "Leaving first thing Saturday morning. Gonna spend the night with one of Preacher's college friends in Tuscaloosa, then go to the rally on Sunday."

"And Reverend Jenkins asked Ma Pearl if I could go?"

Hallelujah released an exasperated sigh as if he were tired of hearing me ask that question. But I couldn't help myself. I had never traveled outside of Stillwater, and now someone was asking me to go all the way to another state — and it wasn't a relative inviting me up north to live. I couldn't help but feel *incredulous,* as my seventh-grade teacher, Miss Johnson, would say.

"Why didn't he ask Papa?" I said. "He would've let me go."

"He did. He spoke to both of them about it last night. Mr. Carter said yes, but Miss Sweet said maybe. She said she needed to think it over."

"I still can't belie—" I stopped myself when I saw the look on Hallelujah's face.

"You said you wished you could do things like that," he said. "So I asked Preacher if you could go with us. And since Aunt Bertha's going, he said yes, if Mr. Carter and Miss Sweet would let you."

I crossed my arms and let out a puff of air. "This is my fault," I said. "I got all worked up over how unfair life was and couldn't think of a decent scripture for Thanksgiving. Now Ma Pearl is holding it against me."

"Life *is* unfair," Hallelujah muttered, his lips barely moving. "Most every race in this country came here on boats. But the African race was the only race brought over here, shackled like animals, in the bottom of the boat."

"Well, I wasn't thinking that far back," I said. "Just to today, and Mr. Robinson giving us that consolation turkey."

Hallelujah laughed. "Consolation turkey?"

"Yep. That's my new name for it. Consolation turkey. A big fat juicy turkey to make up for all the hard work that we don't get paid for."

Hallelujah gestured around the sagging porch and laughed. "Oh, come on now, you get to live in this fine house for free. And what about all that lovely furniture his wife passes along to Miss Sweet? And don't forget the clothes Fred Lee gets when Sam gets tired of wearing them."

I grimaced when I thought about the last time I went to the Robinsons' to pick up a bag of their older son's discarded clothes. It was back in the summer—three days after Levi Jackson was killed. And it was the first time I got to hear how the Robinsons really felt about the NAACP and all this business of integration. Right there in the Robinsons' dining room, Mr. Robinson was holding a meeting of the White Citizens' Council—a group determined to keep Mississippi's Jim Crow status in place. They even referred to the NAACP as the National Association for the "Agitation" of Colored People, and said they were determined to keep them from contaminating the minds of the good colored citizens of Leflore County, Mississippi. How could getting people to strive for a better life be considered contamination?

"Why is it that white people don't want us to have anything?" I asked Hallelujah. "What would be so bad about a Negro family living in a nice house with electricity in every room and a real bathroom on the inside? What would be so bad about a Negro having a house with a hallway in it, or closets to put their clothes in? Or what would even be so bad about a Negro actually going to the store and trying on clothes before they bought them instead of having to look at something and see if it fits? Why can't we try on clothes and shoes like the white folks do? Why do we have to let them draw the shape of our feet on a piece of paper to see if the shoes fit?"

"Because we were brought over, shackled, at the bottom of the boat," Hallelujah answered dryly. "We're beneath them —in their opinion."

Then, as if some alarm had sounded in his head, Hallelujah flinched and eyed me curiously.

"What?" I asked.

"Colored people *do* live in houses with bathrooms and electricity in every room. Some even have hallways and closets." Hallelujah gave me a pitiful stare and said, "You've never seen that, have you?"

I shrugged, embarrassed. "Aunt Clara Jean's house kinda has a bathroom in it. They have a toilet and a tub, but they have to get water from the pump to pour in the back of the toilet to flush it. And they have to fill the tub with pump water because the faucets don't work."

"So good old Mr. Robinson had the bathroom fixtures put in, but he never had the plumbing connected," Hallelujah said, cutting his eyes in the direction of Mr. Robinson's house.

I frowned but didn't answer.

"Didn't your mama and Mr. Pete have those things in their house in Greenwood?" asked Hallelujah.

Again I shrugged. "Me and Fred Lee never set foot in Mama's house in Greenwood."

This time Hallelujah looked embarrassed. "Sorry," he muttered.

"Not your fault," I said. To liven things up, I lightly punched his shoulder and said, "I never been to your house either."

Hallelujah thought for a moment. "You haven't, have you?"

I shook my head. "Nope. I've only been to school, church, and Mr. Robinson's place."

"You've been to more places than that," Hallelujah countered.

"Okay, my aunt's house out in the sticks, where she no longer lives. And to your aunt's store and to the Jamisons' store the few times I've been to town with Papa and Uncle Ollie."

Hallelujah smiled and said, "Well, now we're about to change all that."

"But Ma Pearl won't let me go."

Hallelujah winked. "My aunt is a powerful persuader."

"And you're a good friend," I said, smiling.

"Always."

Feeling guilty, I decided to tell him the truth about my conversation with Shorty.

"You know me and Shorty didn't just talk about my daddy, right?"

Hallelujah nodded. "I know. A boy in my class told me about his plans."

"So you already know what he's planning to do?"

Hallelujah frowned. "Yeah. He asked Edward and a few others to join him. Said they weren't gonna hurt anybody, just scare 'em."

I breathed a sigh of relief. I didn't have to "run 'n tell Jenkins." Someone else already had. "He asked me for Papa's shotgun," I said.

"He asked Edward the same thing. *And* he asked him if they could use his daddy's car. Edward told him he had lost his mind if he thought he was gonna get his daddy's shotgun and ride around in the middle of the night and shoot out white folks' windows." Hallelujah shrugged. "Wouldn't do anything but start a riot anyway."

"You gonna tell your daddy?"

"Nope," Hallelujah said flatly. "Shorty won't do it. He doesn't have the resources. He can't sneak around at night in that loud truck of his." Hallelujah scoffed. "He doesn't have the guts, either."

"Humph. That's what he said about me. But what if he does? What if he can get somebody to help him?"

"That's his problem if he wants to get thrown in jail. Or worse, get shot and killed."

I winced. "Then maybe you *should* tell your daddy."

With a frown, Hallelujah said, "I probably should. But Shorty Cooper doesn't seem to be the kind of fellow who can be reasoned with."

"How do you know if you never talk to him?"

Hallelujah crossed his arms over his chest. He didn't answer me.

I cut my eyes at him and said, "So, Shorty was right."

Hallelujah returned my sideways glance. "Right about what?"

"That you class yourself."

Hallelujah glared at me. "I don't class myself. I just select my friends carefully."

I shook my head. "Same thing."

With a huff, Hallelujah said, "Okay, I'll talk to him."

I smiled. "You'll see. He's not as bad as you think."

Hallelujah groaned.

"So what's *your* plan?" I asked. "You said in Miss Hill's class that we should march or something, like they're doing in the cities. But where will we march? And what good would it do?"

"Marching itself doesn't do anything. But it shows that we're united. It shows how many people want to see change. How many are willing to stand up for their rights."

"You think marching in Stillwater would do any good?"

Hallelujah smirked. "It'd be better than shooting out white folks' windows in the middle of the night."

"Seriously," I said, "what *can* we do? I mean, we *are* just children."

With a smug grin and a tilt of his head, Hallelujah said, "I'm a man, remember?"

I rolled my eyes. "Yeah, a man who's going places. But for now, what're you gonna do while you're still in Mississippi?"

Hallelujah shook his head and said, "I honestly don't know yet. That's why I can't wait to go to Montgomery. I want to hear what Dr. Howard and the others are doing."

"Still thinking about going into a place and demanding to be served?" I teased him. "What about Danny Ray Martin's store? He has that little dinky restaurant in the back where his colored workers cook collard greens and cornbread and serve 'em up to his white customers for lunch."

Hallelujah chuckled. "Don't think that would work. His colored workers would be too scared to serve us anyway. But, hey," he said, smirking, "since Preacher said we needed a Joshua, maybe we could march around the store seven times like the Israelites did with the walls of Jericho."

I raised my hands and pretended to blow a trumpet. "Then we'll blow our trumpets, and the walls will come tumbling down."

We laughed for a moment before the conversation turned serious again.

"What if we really did do that?" Hallelujah asked. "Can you imagine how scared Danny Ray Martin or anyone else would be if a group of colored children silently marched around their store seven times?"

I shook my head and said, "No. They'd just think we were crazy."

"Then let 'em think we're crazy. I think we should do it."

I went silent for a second, thinking about my cousin Mule in Arkansas.

"What's the matter?" Hallelujah asked.

"What if we get arrested for trespassing? What if we go to jail?" I sighed and confessed, "I don't know if I'm ready for any of this. I keep thinking about Mule and how he got beat up in jail." I rubbed my face. "I can't imagine someone hitting me hard enough to break my jaw."

I remembered how Ma Pearl had once slapped me hard enough to knock me from my chair, and how she had socked Aunt Belle in the jaw and knocked her across the room. Neither of us had a broken jaw, but I know for me, the pain from the slap was nearly unbearable.

"Pain is part of the process," Hallelujah said.

"You reading my mind?" I asked.

Hallelujah answered, "No. Your face. It's scrunched up like you just sucked ten lemons."

I relaxed my face and tried to laugh with my friend, even though there was nothing really to laugh about. All that talk about marching now had my stomach in knots. I didn't want to go to jail and get beat up.

Hallelujah extended his hands toward me, palms up. "Give me your hands," he said.

"Why?"

He nodded at his hands. "Just place your hands in mine."

I shrugged and did as I was asked.

"Okay, now say the Twenty-Third Psalm with me."

"What?"

Hallelujah sighed. "Just do it, okay?"

"The Lord is my shepherd," Hallelujah started. "I shall not want. He maketh me to lie down in green pastures."

I joined him at "He leadeth me beside the still waters."

Together we said, "He restoreth my soul. He leadeth me in the path of righteousness, for his name's sake . . ."

But when we got to the part about the valley of the shadow of death, I wouldn't say it.

Hallelujah gave my hands a slight squeeze. "This is the most important part. Yea, though I walk through the valley of the shadow of death," he said. "I will fear no evil."

I shook my head. "No."

"Yea, though I walk through the valley of the shadow of death," he said again.

I thought about all the people who had walked through that valley—Reverend Lee, Levi Jackson, Lamar Smith, Emmett Till. They had not survived.

I snatched my hands from Hallelujah's grip.

He grabbed my hands. "I will fear no evil."

I tried to pull away, but Hallelujah held on tightly.

"Please let go of my hands," I said. My voice cracked. "I do fear evil."

With his eyes full of concern, Hallelujah asked, "Don't you believe God will protect you?"

I shook my head and answered, "No."

Hallelujah sighed and let go of my hands.

When tears sprang to my eyes, Hallelujah placed his arm around my shoulders and said he was sorry.

I nodded and tried to say it was okay, but I was too choked up to speak.

I felt weak. Like a failure. There I was, standing beside one of the bravest boys I knew, and I couldn't even recite a scripture with him. I couldn't say out loud, "I will fear no evil, for thou art with me."

Because whether God was with me or not, I feared evil.

Folks said that when Willie Reed testified against Roy Bryant and J. W. Milam, he told the court that he heard screams coming out of the barn where they were beating Emmett Till. He said he heard Emmett Till screaming for his mama.

After Willie Reed testified and was immediately spirited off to Chicago, it was said that he had a nervous breakdown.

Everyone fears evil.

After I calmed down, I asked Hallelujah, "How can you not be afraid?"

"I am afraid," he said. "But I'm willing to walk through the valley in spite of my fears."

When the front door creaked open, we both jumped. Hallelujah quickly removed his arm from my shoulders.

Miss Bertha peered through the screen door. After an awkward glance at us, she stepped outside and smiled. "I have some good news," she said.

Chapter Fourteen

SATURDAY, NOVEMBER 26

I COULDN'T BELIEVE I WAS ACTUALLY GOING TO Montgomery, Alabama. It almost made up for the disappointment of my daddy not showing up for Thanksgiving.

No one, or nothing, had to wake me that morning—not Ma Pearl, not our old halfway faithful rooster, Slick Charlie, not even the angel Gabriel bringing the sun from the other side of the world and hanging it over Stillwater. In fact, I doubt I even slept more than two hours the whole night. I don't know how they did it, but Reverend Jenkins and Miss Bertha's convincing Ma Pearl to let me go to Alabama was the best thing that ever happened to me. Maybe being around a bunch of brave people in Montgomery would help me be braver.

It was still dark outside, but I had already washed up and dressed myself using the light from the kerosene lamp. Even Queen couldn't sleep. She sat on the side of her bed wanting to know what she could help me with. I almost felt like I was in a dream. Queen had never been nice to me in my life. Never. Not even the night I helped wipe her wounds after

Ma Pearl beat her when she found out she'd been sneaking out of the house at night.

But in the early-morning dimness I could even see a smile on her face. Was she happy I was going to Alabama, or just happy I wasn't going to be around for a few days?

"It's too bad Baby Susta didn't bring you no new clothes this summer," Queen said, yawning and halfway covering her mouth with her palm.

"I was able to borrow a couple of dresses from Miss Bertha," I said.

Queen shrugged. "I know. But they ain't city clothes. They Mississippi clothes."

"Miss Bertha buys her clothes in Greenwood. She has nice things."

Queen waved her hand. "I don't mean that. Old man Jamison got *nice* things in his store right here in Stillwater, but they ain't like the clothes from Saint Louis."

I glanced down at the dress Miss Bertha had loaned me. It might not have come from Saint Louis, but it was the most fashionable outfit I had ever worn. I smoothed down the front of the navy blue dress with the palms of my hands. It's a good thing Miss Bertha was tall and slender. The dress was a perfect fit for me. And so were the black patent leather shoes. But my legs were bare. Ma Pearl said stockings would have given me the big head and made me think I was grown.

I had two more of Miss Bertha's dresses packed in the brown suitcase Hallelujah let me borrow. One was pink and the other brown. I didn't think I would look good in brown, so I would wear the pink one to Dexter Avenue Baptist Church, where Dr. Howard was speaking. I wanted to look my best. I wanted to look like I belonged in a crowd of sophisticated Negroes. I wanted to have the confidence that Saint Louis girl, Ophelia the Ogre, had when she visited with Aunt Belle over the summer.

"Rose Lee!" Ma Pearl called from Fred Lee's room. "You ready? Preacher 'n 'em be here in a lil' bit."

After a few squeaks of the floorboards, I heard her say to Fred Lee, "Git up, boy. Yo' sister 'bout to leave. Make sho' you tell her bye."

Ma Pearl made it sound like I was leaving forever. I was only going to be gone until early Monday morning. Reverend Jenkins was planning to get back in time for school, but there was no way he could do that if the meeting was late in the day. So he said he'd figure it all out when we got there. If we missed school for one more day, it wouldn't hurt too much, he'd said.

Ma Pearl pulled back the curtain that separated our room from Fred Lee's. "You ready, gal?"

"Yes, ma'am." I pointed at the packed suitcase.

Ma Pearl glanced at the suitcase, then at Queen. "You up

too? You need to lay on back down 'n rest. You go'n lose 'nuff sleep when that baby come. No sense skimpin' on it now." She turned to me and said, "You come on in here and git somethin' to eat. Preacher 'n 'em ain't go'n 'cuse me o' sendin' you on the road hungry."

"Fret'Lee, go git that gal's suitcase and carr' it to the parlor," she said as she lumbered back through the house.

Even Aunt Ruthie was waiting for me in the kitchen. Since all her children were still asleep, she enjoyed breakfast and coffee with Papa and me. I ate three biscuits and a plate of grits and eggs and chugged down two cups of coffee while savoring the company of Papa and Aunt Ruthie. Ma Pearl warned me that the coffee would run right through me and began chastising me ahead of time for making Reverend Jenkins have to pull over on the side of the road just so I could pee. I assured her it wouldn't happen seeing how many times I had drunk two cups of coffee before going to work in the cotton field, and I had never had to stop to do my business before it was time for a break.

After eating, I quickly washed up and sat in the chair near the window of the parlor and listened for the sound of Reverend Jenkins's Buick to pull into the yard. Slick Charlie had crowed minutes before. And now old faithful Gabriel was bringing the sun to set it in the sky over Stillwater.

"Preacher shoulda been here by now," Ma Pearl said as

she entered the parlor, wiping her hands on the tail of her apron.

Papa nodded toward the window, where daylight was finally showing through. "He'll be here in a minute. He had to get Bertha, too. Womens can be slow sometimes."

Ma Pearl grunted and said, "Mens too." She spun on her heels and left the room.

Papa and I sat and sat, waiting for Reverend Jenkins to show up. We waited for so long that Aunt Ruthie's children got up and about, and the two boys went outside to play.

The parlor had begun to grow warm, so I opened the window to let in the little breeze that was stirring outside, swirling leaves around in the yard. I don't know why it mattered at that point, but I figured opening the window would help me hear better when the Buick pulled up. It was taking them so long that I had begun to panic, thinking that perhaps they showed up while we were sitting around the table chatting over coffee. What if they came and knocked quietly because they thought everyone besides me and perhaps Papa was sleeping, and they didn't want to wake them? What if I had missed my one chance to travel and hear a great man speak?

Papa must have read my thoughts by the look on my face. "Somethin' musta happened," he said, his voice a bit croaky. "Preacher don't run this late, no matter what."

My palms began to sweat. What if they left me on

purpose? What if they forgot me? Surely Hallelujah wouldn't forget me. And Miss Bertha was so excited for me to come so she could have a female companion along for the ride that she brought those dresses over for me later the same day. Maybe someone important, like an NAACP worker, asked to go and took my place. My heart sank at the thought.

Ma Pearl entered the parlor and smirked. "You still thank Bertha holdin' 'em up?"

Papa shook his head. "This ain't like Preacher. He ain't never late."

"Humph," Ma Pearl countered. "I'on know what church you been goin' to, but that boy been late mo' times than I can count on both hands."

Papa only shook his head again and repeated, "This ain't like Preacher. He ain't never late."

"Well, he late today," Ma Pearl retorted.

As soon as the words passed her lips, rocks crunched on the road.

I jumped up from my chair. "They're here!"

Papa calmed me down. "Hold on, daughter. Ain't proper for a lady to rush out the do' that way. They'll come up and knock."

I sighed and slumped down in the chair. I had waited for hours. I guess it wouldn't hurt to wait another minute for Hallelujah to come to the door.

When not just one but two car doors slammed, I peered out the window. Both Hallelujah and Reverend Jenkins were coming toward the porch. From my position, I could barely see into the car. But it appeared to be empty. I couldn't believe they still hadn't picked up Miss Bertha.

Papa squinted at me when I opened the door before anyone knocked. I could tell he wanted to say something, but before he could, Hallelujah was inside the door. Reverend Jenkins spilled in right behind him.

From the looks on their faces, I just knew something bad had happened to Shorty. I just knew he'd gone out and gotten himself killed.

My hands, which were already sweaty, started to shake.

"Preacher?" Papa inquired.

With a grim look, Reverend Jenkins shook his head. His voice quivered when he spoke. "God help us, Mr. Carter. These crackers done shot Gus Courts."

Chapter Fifteen

SATURDAY, NOVEMBER 26

My tense shoulders slumped in relief when Reverend Jenkins didn't mention Shorty. But whoever Gus Courts was, his being shot was a cause of tears for Reverend Jenkins. He had barely slumped down on the settee before he removed his glasses, dropped his head in his palms, and began bawling like a small child. I had never seen him cry, not even at a funeral.

Papa and I both turned to Hallelujah for answers. But he only sat beside his father and placed his arm around his shaking shoulders. "It's okay, Papa," he said. "At least he's not dead."

Papa. I had never heard Hallelujah refer to Reverend Jenkins as anything other than Preacher. He said it's because that's what he grew up hearing everyone else call him. But Papa. That's what he called him in his heart.

"Hallelujah, what—"

With his palm raised, Papa cut me off before I could utter another word. He shook his head. The look on his face said, "Not yet, daughter."

I sat back in my chair by the window, and Papa sat in the matching chair near the door. I don't know what was on Papa's mind, but I was praying that Ma Pearl wouldn't come barging into the parlor being loud and rude. I didn't want her seeing Reverend Jenkins at such a low point.

I had so many questions, but I couldn't ask any.

Who was Gus Courts?

Where was Miss Bertha?

And were we still going to Montgomery, Alabama?

I certainly couldn't gather the answer to my last question by the way Reverend Jenkins and Hallelujah were dressed. They always dressed as if they had somewhere important to go. But since Miss Bertha wasn't with them and we were supposed to leave for Montgomery two hours earlier, I had to assume we weren't going. My heart felt like it deflated.

These crackers done shot Gus Courts. Now, *crackers* wasn't even a word Reverend Jenkins used. And with him being an English teacher, he certainly, under normal circumstances, wouldn't have said "done" instead of "have."

When Aunt Ruthie appeared at the parlor door, her eyes rounded and her mouth fell into an O. I could tell she was embarrassed to see Reverend Jenkins crying by the way she hurriedly backed out of the doorway. I followed her into the front room to explain, and to see whether she knew who Gus Courts was.

She didn't. She had never heard the name, either.

"Could it be someone kin to them?" I asked.

Aunt Ruthie shook her head. "I ain't never see'd Preacher cry. He didn't cry at his own papa's funeral."

"His mama's?" I inquired.

"She died when he was a boy."

Chills covered my arms. "Just like Hallelujah," I said quietly. "He never told me that."

"Preacher ain't no emotional man," Aunt Ruthie said, her eyes sad. "He don't cry easy."

"Where's Ma Pearl?" I whispered.

"Out in the toilet," answered Aunt Ruthie.

"Good," I said, touching Aunt Ruthie's arm. "I don't want her to see Reverend Jenkins like this."

Aunt Ruthie rolled her eyes. "Lawd knows we don't need that."

When I came back to the parlor, Reverend Jenkins was wiping his face with a handkerchief.

Hallelujah peered up at me. "We took Aunt Bertha to Mound Bayou," he said. "She's safer there."

I gave him a puzzled look.

"Gus Courts was shot yesterday while he was checking receipts at the cash register in his store down in Belzoni."

Belzoni. That's the same town where Reverend George

Lee, back in May, was shot and killed for helping colored people register to vote.

Noticing the look on my face, Hallelujah nodded and said, "He was a friend of Reverend Lee. Like him, he was helping other Negroes register to vote."

Papa finally spoke. "Y'all think Bertha might be in danger?"

Reverend Jenkins cleared his throat and said, "We're all in danger, Mr. Carter." His voice was choked but strong. "When someone is evil enough to gun down a sixty-five-year-old man who was only trying to do right by his community, it tells me that none of our lives matter to them."

"*Sixty-five?*" asked Papa.

"Two years older than Lamar Smith, who was gunned down in August," said Hallelujah.

Lamar Smith. A sixty-three-year-old farmer and war veteran had been shot down at the courthouse in a city called Brookhaven.

He was killed in broad daylight.

His killer, they say, walked away from the scene, covered in Lamar Smith's blood.

The sheriff stood by and watched it all happen.

He did nothing.

Lamar Smith's crime? Helping Negroes register to vote.

Just like this man, Gus Courts. And just like his friend Reverend George Lee.

May. June. July. *August.* September. October. *November.* It seemed that if Negros continued helping other Negroes register to vote, a Negro would get gunned down every three months.

Shorty's words rang in my ears. *"Them dirty dogs done shot down a sixty-three-year-old man . . . Who go'n be next? Somebody's granmama?"*

I didn't know if I could keep dealing with this evil.

"He still alive, you say?" Papa asked.

"Barely," answered Reverend Jenkins. "But he's lucky for that even. He insisted they take him to Dr. Battle in Indianola. He sent him straight to Mound Bayou for surgery. He knew they'd probably let him die at Humphreys County Memorial. White surgeons won't try to save a colored man, especially when he's the head of the local NAACP."

"Is that where they took the preacher?" Papa asked.

Reverend Jenkins shook his head. "Reverend Lee never made it to the hospital. He died before he got there."

"Sorry we can't go to Montgomery," Hallelujah said to me. "I know how much it meant to you."

I smiled and shrugged that it was okay. But it wasn't. My heart ached for Mr. Gus Courts and his family, if he had one.

But it ached even more for myself. Tears threatened to rush to my eyes. But I fought them. Reverend Jenkins had cried enough for all of us that day.

"Bertha's too distraught to travel," he said. "She decided to stay in Mound Bayou with a friend for a while. Those crackers wouldn't dare cross the line over there and start trouble."

There was that word again. I had never seen Reverend Jenkins upset enough to use a derogatory term to describe any race of people.

"What's go'n happen when she come back?" Papa asked.

Reverend Jenkins shook his head. "I don't want her to come back. I might have to pick up my own gun if these crackers hurt my sister."

This time I cringed when the word *cracker* came from Reverend Jenkins's mouth. He was always saying that just because white folks used derogatory names to try to degrade us did not mean we had to sling ugly names back at them— not that any colored person would have called a white person *cracker* or *peckerwood* or *redneck* to his face and lived. But what Reverend Jenkins hated even more was when colored people used the derogatory names to describe themselves.

"I s'pose nobody saw who did it," said Papa.

Reverend Jenkins tried to snicker at Papa's sarcasm, but he was too full of sadness and what came out of his mouth was a cross between a laugh and a moan. "There are always witnesses, Mr. Carter," he said. "But we both know they'll never talk."

Like a ghost, Ma Pearl suddenly appeared in the doorway. With her size, it was amazing that she was able to sneak up without being noticed.

"What's goin' on?" she asked. "Where Bertha?"

"Another shootin', Pearl," said Papa. "A grocery store owner in Belzoni."

"Bertha shot?" Ma Pearl asked, her eyes wide.

"No, not Bertha, Miss Sweet," said Reverend Jenkins. "Gus Courts down in Belzoni."

Ma Pearl threw up her hands and headed over to the sofa. "I asted y'all 'bout Bertha, and y'all tell me some sto' owner been shot. How the devil I s'pose to know the difference?"

She let out a heavy sigh as she sank into the sofa. The poor sofa creaked under her weight. She crossed her arms over her bosom and said, "Now who got shot again?"

"Gus Courts. A store owner in Belzoni," said Papa.

"Who shot him?" Ma Pearl asked matter-of-factly.

"Some think it might be the head of their local White Citizens' Council," answered Reverend Jenkins.

Ma Pearl snorted. "I bet he messin' with them NAACP peoples, ain't he?"

When no one answered, Ma Pearl shook her head and

said, "I told you them folks ain't doin' nothin' but gittin' good peoples kil't."

When the rest of us still said nothing, Ma Pearl squinted at Reverend Jenkins. "Preacher, I'on' mean no harm," she said. "But I really don't want y'all bringin' that mess up in my house no mo'. Too many peoples gittin' shot, and Mr. Robinson done already told us we gots to go if we start involving ourselves with them peoples. I ain't got nowhere else to go, 'specially now that I got a whole house full o' folks living here. And I sho' don't wanna mess around and git myself shot."

Reverend Jenkins gave Ma Pearl an up-and-down look. "I don't think you have anything to worry about, Miss Sweet. I doubt that someone like you poses a threat to the White Citizens' Council goal to preserve their segregated South."

Luckily the teakettle let out a whistle and summoned Ma Pearl back to the kitchen. Otherwise, I think Reverend Jenkins might have landed in 1956 before the rest of us got there. Ma Pearl had that look on her face that said she was about to slap him straight on into the next year.

December

Chapter Sixteen

SATURDAY, DECEMBER 3

Dᴇᴄᴇᴍʙᴇʀ ᴄᴀᴍᴇ ɪɴ ᴄᴏʟᴅ, ᴡᴇᴛ, ᴀɴᴅ ɢʟᴏᴏᴍʏ. Aɴᴅ it wasn't gloomy simply because the sun had been hiding behind rain-soaked clouds for two days straight. It was gloomy because I couldn't stop thinking about what a fool I had been to stay in Mississippi—a place where old men were shot just for wanting to vote. When Reverend Jenkins finally had a chance to talk to Mr. Gus Courts after his surgery, he said he told him that all he wanted was a chance to vote before he died—a chance to feel like he had the rights of a citizen in Mississippi. He said, "The Negro pays taxes, so why can't he vote?" I didn't know much about taxes, but I surely hadn't heard of any white folks trying to gun down Negroes for paying them.

Sixty-five. That's how old Gus Courts was. Papa was fifty-nine, and he said he was too old to concern himself with voting. Though I loved my grandfather dearly, for the first time in my life I felt ashamed of him for not being bold like Gus Courts and Lamar Smith. I knew I shouldn't have felt that way, seeing that Lamar Smith was dead and Gus Courts had barely won the battle for his life. But I did feel that way. And the feeling itself somehow embarrassed me. Because I, too, was afraid like Papa. I was afraid to face death for the sake of fairness.

Despite the chilly, damp weather, I sat on the front porch that Saturday morning and brooded. I should have allowed Aunt Belle to return and get me back in November. I should have never written her that letter. Why on earth did I ever think I was brave enough to handle the Jim Crow South? Back when Aunt Belle and Monty were here, their presence gave me strength. But without them, I was no longer Rosa, like the dew in the morning gently refreshing the earth as Monty said. I had gone back to being plain old Rose, the girl who was afraid—the girl who wanted to run away from those miserable cotton fields.

Who was I fooling? Montgomery, Alabama? To hear a rich colored man like Dr. T. R. M. Howard speak? Me and my borrowed dresses packed in my borrowed suitcase? My own grandma wouldn't even allow me to wear a pair of stockings because she didn't want me to get "beside myself."

I would never get to go anywhere, or do anything important. And it was my own fault.

I stared at the red and gold leaves still clinging to the trees. Even their beauty couldn't cheer me. My eyes kept dropping to the ground, at the dead brown leaves scattered across the front yard instead.

When I heard a car stirring up rocks on the road, I glanced up. It was Reverend Jenkins, and surprisingly, Hallelujah was driving. When they pulled into the yard, I tried to smile but couldn't. I had begun to associate their arrival with bad news. I still had heard nothing of Shorty, nor had I seen him in school. I said a silent prayer, hoping the Jenkinses weren't bringing bad news about him.

Hallelujah started waving before he exited the car. I couldn't tell if he was happy to see me or just happy that he was driving. But the smile he wore was bright enough to light up a cloudy night. Of course, he wasn't delivering bad news. A smile like that could never come from a sad heart. From the porch, I waved back at him and found my own smile.

When Hallelujah rushed from the car and raced toward the steps, his jubilance made me giggle. "What's the hurry?" I asked. "We ate all the breakfast, and Ma Pearl don't cook supper on Saturday. So I sure hope you ain't rushing up here for something to eat."

Hallelujah shook his head. "Nope. We came to get *you*," he said, pointing at me.

"Me?" I asked, leaning back in my chair, pointing at myself.

"Yes, you, Rosa Lee Carter," Hallelujah said, nodding. "We're going to Mound Bayou, and you're going with us."

"Moun—" The words stuck in my throat. Mound Bayou? The town where folks said only colored people lived? The place where Dr. T. R. M. Howard was a surgeon and supposedly lived in a mansion that could rival Mr. Robinson's? How was I going? And why?

I didn't allow my hopes to rise. Instead I shook my head and said I couldn't go.

Just as Hallelujah sat in the chair next to me on the porch, Reverend Jenkins reached the front steps. "We didn't take a detour and drive out here for nothing," he said. "We owe you a trip, and you're gonna take it."

"Ma Pearl—"

Hallelujah cut me off. "He's asking Mr. Carter *only*."

"We're visiting Bertha," said Reverend Jenkins. "And you're coming with us."

I smiled and allowed my hopes to rise.

Fifteen minutes later I found myself wearing the pink dress and the black patent leather shoes Miss Bertha had given me as well as a pair of stockings Queen let me borrow. And yes, I was beside myself, just as Ma Pearl had predicted. Yet to keep me from fully "classing myself," she made me wear my ratty brown coat with the too-short sleeves.

Still, I was happy. I was in the back seat of Reverend Jenkins's car (he was now behind the wheel, and not Hallelujah), and I was headed to Mound Bayou, Mississippi. For the first time in my thirteen years of living, I was leaving Stillwater.

Chapter Seventeen

SATURDAY, DECEMBER 3

I REMEMBER ONCE, WHEN I WAS ABOUT ELEVEN YEARS old, I asked Mama if I could go to Greenwood with her. Often when she, Mr. Pete, Sugar, and Lil' Man would come to visit, they would giggle and grin about the games they had played along the drive.

I Spy. That was the name of one of the games. And sometimes they would continue playing it even after they had reached the house.

"I spy with my little eye . . . something green," Mama said.

"A leaf!" Sugar cried.

Mama grinned slyly and pointed at the bottom of the tree. "Fooled ya," she said. "It's the stuff on the bottom of the tree."

I smiled and said, "It's called moss."

Mama frowned at me and quit playing the game.

After that they never again continued their games once they reached our house. Though the games sounded silly and pointless, they made me long to go for a car ride along the highway just the same. Now, two years later, I was finally in a car, riding along the highway, but I knew I was too old to play a game called I Spy with Hallelujah and Reverend Jenkins. Besides, there wasn't much to see except harvested cotton fields. And every town we drove through looked the same —like Stillwater. I don't know what I expected, but I was a little disappointed that I discovered nothing new on the drive from Stillwater to Mound Bayou.

But driving into Mound Bayou was totally different. Not only did it look different, it felt different. It felt safe.

"Here we are," Reverend Jenkins called from the front seat. "Mound Bayou. Mississippi's all-Negro town. Founded by Negroes. Run by Negroes."

Hallelujah peered back at me from the front passenger seat and smiled. I smiled back.

Reverend Jenkins continued. "The late, great Booker T. Washington himself once praised Mound Bayou as a place where a Negro can get inspiration by seeing what other members of his race have accomplished."

Booker T. Washington was a name Miss Johnson had mentioned often, but there was nothing written about him in our history texts. Miss Johnson said he was so smart that he advised presidents even though he himself had been born a slave. I supposed Mrs. Robinson and her church club had never heard of him, since they felt that colored children couldn't learn as fast as white children.

"And I agree with Mr. Washington," Hallelujah chimed

in. He gestured toward the window. "You see these stores? Negro-owned. Every last one of them." He turned to me and grinned. "If that doesn't convince you that colored people can do the same things as whites, I don't know what will."

As Reverend Jenkins's car slowly cruised down a main street, it wasn't the stores that I took note of. It was the people. They all looked the same. They all had brown skin. Like me. And they all walked together on the sidewalk—no one was stepping aside so someone of a lighter color could have more space.

I gasped as we approached what looked like houses but, in my small frame of mind, couldn't have been because they were much too large.

"Are those houses?" I asked.

"Yes, they are," Reverend Jenkins said. He pointed at a two-story brick home and said, "That's the former home of Mary Booze, one of the daughters of the city's founding fathers. The house next to it is the former home of Isaiah Tecumseh Montgomery himself, the man who founded this fine city. That's where the lucky teachers in this city now get to live."

"Teachers have a special house?" I asked.

"A lot of small towns provide for their teachers this way," said Reverend Jenkins. "But Stillwater doesn't. That's why most of us have more than one job. Can't make a living teaching in these small towns."

I thought about how Shorty had mocked Miss Hill for having to chop cotton like the rest of us during the summer. I felt even more sorry for her and wished Stillwater had a home specifically for teachers so she wouldn't have to labor in the field like the rest of us common colored folk. "That's a spectacular house," I said, admiring the sprawling three-story brick structure with its white columns. "If I could live like this, I wouldn't care about going north."

Reverend Jenkins glanced at me in the rearview mirror but said nothing.

"Did I say something wrong?" I asked.

He called over the seat, "Sweetheart, our people are fleeing even a city like Mound Bayou in favor the North. They can't stay cocooned within the safety of this city forever. At some point, they have to venture out into the Jim Crow South with the rest of us. And it's that venturing out that scares people and makes them fear for their lives."

"But Dr. Howard is here," I offered. "He's not going anywhere, is he?"

"No time soon, I hope," Reverend Jenkins replied. "Besides, he came from up north. Well, I shouldn't say up north," he added. "He was born in Kentucky, but he's lived up north and various other places around the country. His last home was Nashville. But he's here now, and we're lucky to have him."

"Hey," Hallelujah pointed, as if to divert attention away from the current subject. "The Banks house."

I raised myself slightly in my seat to have a look. Before me sat another beautiful house in which I couldn't believe a colored person could possibly live. "Did you say Banks?"

"Yes," said Hallelujah. "Mr. Charles Banks."

"Humph, wonder if he's related to me," I said under my breath.

"What's that, Rosa?" Reverend Jenkins called over the seat.

"Nothing," I muttered. Though Reverend Jenkins and Hallelujah knew all about my daddy and how he wasn't a part of mine or Fred Lee's life, I was still embarrassed whenever he was mentioned around them.

"Mr. Banks was from Clarksdale," Reverend Jenkins offered. "He moved here shortly after the city was founded and opened, quite fittingly, the Bank of Mound Bayou."

I continued to stare out the window and wonder at that marvel called Mound Bayou, a place where a Negro was as free as a white person. My eyes bugged out as we came near a large red-brick building. "Is that a *church?*"

"Sure is," said Reverend Jenkins. "First Baptist Church."

"It's brick!" I gasped. "And it's bigger than Second Baptist in Stillwater."

Reverend Jenkins chuckled. "It was probably built before that one, too. It's supposedly the first brick church ever built in this area."

"Wow," I whispered. "I wonder what Mrs. Robinson and her Cackling Church Club would think of a colored church that was bigger than theirs *and* was called First Baptist instead of Second."

Reverend Jenkins laughed heartily this time. "And I'm sure they have no idea that one of the very *first* Second Baptist churches was started by former slaves in the North."

"Really?" I said, sitting a bit straighter in my seat.

"Yep. And it was also one of the stopping points on the Underground Railroad," said Reverend Jenkins. "Right up there in Detroit."

"How interesting," I said. "That's the same place they caused Levi's family to run off to."

"Maybe we should tell them all this," Hallelujah joked.

Reverend Jenkins shook his head. "Nah. Ignorance is bliss. Let 'em be happy."

"One of the ladies in Mrs. Robinson's Bible study *implied* that colored children aren't as smart as white children so we shouldn't want to go to the same schools," I said. "I bet all of 'em would be surprised if they came here and saw these fine houses and that fancy brick church."

Reverend Jenkins's hearty laugh seemed to rock the Buick. "Not as smart, huh?" he said, his shoulders shaking from his laughter. "Well, wouldn't they be surprised to know that one of their very own, Mr. Joseph Davis, and his brother Jefferson Davis, believed their slaves were so smart that they taught them not only to read and write but also how to run their plantations."

Hallelujah and I shouted at the same time, "They did?"

"Sure did," said Reverend Jenkins. "Benjamin Montgomery, father of one of the men who founded this city, was owned by Joseph Davis. The story goes that old Ben ran away. When Mr. Davis captured him, he asked him why he was so dissatisfied that he would run away. Old Ben told him he wasn't happy being treated like property instead of a person. So Mr. Davis made an agreement with him to treat him like a fellow human being, and the first thing he did was take old Ben out of the cotton field and put him in charge of his general store."

"A slave ran a white man's store?" Hallelujah inquired.

"Yes, he did," Reverend Jenkins said, nodding. "And that was only the beginning. When Mr. Davis saw how well old Ben handled his store, he put him in charge of all the purchasing and shipping on his large plantation. And when old Ben's son Isaiah, the one who founded this city, was born, Mr. Davis made sure he received a proper education too. So you just tell *Miz* Robinson and her Second Baptist church friends that Mr. Joseph Davis thought Negroes were smart enough to run his plantation and handle his money."

I laughed and said, "Reverend Jenkins, you know I can't say that to Mrs. Robinson." Then, in a voice like Ma Pearl's, I said, "We'd git thowed right off her place."

The car roared with laughter.

After the laughter died down, I asked a bit more about the city. "How did it get started?"

Reverend Jenkins sat a bit straighter. "Well, long before the war that freed the slaves was ever fought, folks said that Joseph Davis and his brother Jefferson were already thinking perhaps Negroes could actually be enterprising and run their own towns."

"Really?" Hallelujah interrupted. "A slave owner thought like that?"

Reverend Jenkins nodded. "They even allowed their slaves to work outside the plantation and keep whatever money they earned.

With a raised finger, Hallelujah interjected. "But didn't they have to reimburse the slave owner for their time off the plantation?"

"Oh, definitely," said Reverend Jenkins. "Just the same, folks say that old Ben actually accumulated wealth and opened his own store—Montgomery and Sons—with his son, Isaiah. It was actually Ben's dream to establish a community of freed slaves, but he died before his dream came to fruition. His son, Isaiah, with his cousin Benjamin Green and a few other freed slaves, purchased this land and established the city of Mound Bayou."

"So the Davises were good slave owners?" I asked.

Reverend Jenkins began laughing so hard that I thought he'd have to pull the car to the side of the road. When he finally composed himself, he glanced at me in the rearview mirror and said, "Sweetheart, there's no such thing as a good slave owner. Joseph and Jefferson Davis might have been good *to* their slaves, but there's nothing good about buying and selling your fellow human beings and owning them as if they were cattle."

"How come you never told me all this stuff about the Davises and old Ben?" Hallelujah asked.

"You never asked," answered Reverend Jenkins. "You're not as inquisitive as Rosa," he added, laughing playfully.

"It's because of my name," I said. "Aunt Belle's fiancé, Monty, said it's Italian, after a saint, Rose of Viterbo. He said the bearers of the name tend to analyze the world. And we search for deeper truths than what's simply on the surface."

"Well, I'll be," said Reverend Jenkins. "That sure does sound like you."

"Hmmm," said Hallelujah. "I wonder what Clyde means."

"I don't know what Clyde means, but I know *hallelujah* means 'praise ye the Lord,'" said Reverend Jenkins.

I snickered when I thought about how coarse Hallelujah's words could get when he was angry. I didn't know all that much about names and such, but I did know I wanted to learn as much as I could about a town that was founded by ex-slaves whose masters taught them to read, write, and figure mathematics.

I gestured toward the houses and shops lining the main street in Mound Bayou. "How come they don't write about *this* in the history books?"

Reverend Jenkins glanced at me briefly, then chortled.

Hallelujah answered my question. "They don't want us to know that our people are smart. They want us to think they were all just dumb slaves who were incapable of learning. Who wouldn't appear dumb after they've been captured and brought to a strange land where they don't speak the language?"

Silence filled the car. *Captured and brought to a strange land where they don't speak the language.* I always knew that slaves came from Africa. But I had never really given much thought to how hard it must have been for the first slaves

—brought over on ships like cargo, separated from their families, sold to people who made them live in shacks and work all day in fields, then whipped them if they didn't. I wonder how many whippings some of the slaves got simply because they couldn't understand the instructions given by their owners. I shivered at the thought.

"Slavery was horrible," I said quietly.

The car was quiet again, and I felt badly because it seemed I had spoiled our good mood. But by the time we toured the main streets in Mound Bayou, drove a little way out into the country, and arrived at the home of Miss Bertha's friend, I was—as Mr. Booker T. Washington predicted—inspired.

Then my stomach clenched like a fist.

I was outside of Stillwater. Off Mr. Robinson's place. Not at school. Not at Aunt Clara Jean's. Not at Aunt Ruthie's. Not in Miss Bertha's store. I was sitting in the back seat of a car, which was parked in the driveway of a home of people who were probably as sophisticated as the Saint Louis spectators who had visited with Aunt Belle back in the summer. The house wasn't as huge as the houses we had seen earlier, but it was larger than any colored person's house I had ever seen. And it was painted white, unlike most of the houses I had seen in my lifetime, which had no paint at all.

The white house was accented by green—the shutters surrounding the windows, the front door, shrubs surrounding the house, and a couple of evergreen trees. Even with winter approaching, the green surrounding the house seemed to make it warm and inviting.

Regardless, I began to panic. Who was I to go in there and meet Miss Bertha's friends? And what if she complimented me on how nice I looked in *her* dress? My armpits moistened with sweat, and the sweat rolled down my sides. I prayed it didn't show through the pink fabric of my borrowed dress. I would simply die.

Chapter Eighteen

SATURDAY, DECEMBER 3

W<small>E WERE BARELY OUT OF THE CAR WHEN</small> M<small>ISS</small> Bertha appeared at the door. She smiled brightly and waved big.

"Y'all come on in," she called.

Hallelujah raced up to the door and grabbed his aunt in a hug. He squeezed her as if he hadn't seen her in years. And from my perspective, it seemed Miss Bertha was squeezing him as equally hard.

Reverend Jenkins strolled up to her. "How ya doin', sis?" he asked as he gave her a quick peck on her cheek.

Miss Bertha hugged him and said, "I'm ready to go home. Ready to get back to my store."

Reverend Jenkins shook his head. "I told you I don't want to have to hurt anybody in Stillwater. So unless you want to see your old brother behind bars, you best stay here where it's safe."

"I'm not gonna let those people keep me from my store," Miss Bertha answered as she led us inside the house. "They've tried to destroy it a hundred times already, and I haven't let that scare me into shutting it down. So there's no point in being scared now. I might as well face my fears and get back home."

"We'll see," Reverend Jenkins answered. He stood to the side and allowed us all to enter first.

I trailed behind Miss Bertha, actually wishing I could somehow disappear. I tugged my ratty coat closed as if that might somehow hide it — as if no one would notice where the cloth on the sleeves had rolled into tiny balls like white polka dots on brown fabric.

We entered what I recognized as a foyer — a cozy, narrow hallway for welcoming visitors. The Robinsons had one. I couldn't believe I was in a colored home that had one, too. The floor was a glossy dark wood, the walls, a welcoming shade of green, like the rind of a muskmelon. Framed photos sat atop a dark wood table, and above the table was a mirror framed in gold. I hurried past it before I dared catch a reflection of myself and spoil the moment.

To the right of the foyer was a dining room. It was as lovely as the Robinsons', with a cherry wood table and a matching china cabinet. To the left of the foyer was a living room. Miss Bertha motioned us toward it and said to make ourselves comfortable.

And comfortable I was. My shoes seemed to sink right into the stuff I knew to be carpet. The Robinsons' bedroom floors were covered with it. But since I was never actually allowed inside any of the bedrooms, I had never felt this stuff called carpet before. It didn't feel the same as walking on the rugs in the parlor and dining room. It felt more like walking on a thick layer of fallen leaves.

The room was so green. And vibrant. Green velvet furniture. Green walls. And green plants in pots that sat upon shiny, unscratched tables at the ends of the long sofa. Framed family photos dressed the walls. We had family photos on the walls, too. But there were no frames. Tacks held them in place.

A smile spread across my face at the thought that colored people in the Mississippi Delta lived in houses like this. I could easily imagine a picture of this room on a page of *Jet* magazine. Then I thought about folks like Levi Jackson's family, who had for years lived in that decrepit old house on Mr. Robinson's place before they moved to Detroit after Levi was killed in July. Or Aunt Ruthie, whose house was so cold in winter that she and her children, even though huddled around the woodstove, still wore their coats to keep warm. And poor old Miss Addie—she lived in that three-room shack where a huge tree trunk grew right through the middle of her front-room floor. Thinking of her almost turned my smile to sadness, until a beautiful girl appeared in the doorway and asked if we wanted something to drink.

The girl had long, thick hair, curled in ringlets. Her complexion was like cocoa, and I couldn't help noticing the loveliness of her features. She reminded me of something I had read in the Song of Solomon: *I am black, but comely.* And if I recalled correctly, Reverend Jenkins had said *comely* meant "lovely and pleasant to look at." And that's what this girl was: black, lovely, and pleasant to look at. Just like Aunt Ruthie.

Reverend Jenkins leaped from his seat. "Lord, is this little miss Joe with an *e*?" he asked.

The girl grinned and said, "I prefer Joe Ann, now. Thank you very much." She crossed her arms and declared, "Besides, I'm sixteen. I'm not little anymore!"

Joe Ann, with an *e*?

Like me, she had both a girl's name and a boy's name, except hers sounded pretty. I never liked that I had my daddy's middle name, Lee. It was fine for my brother, Fred Lee. But I always thought it sounded strange on me, a girl — Rose Lee. I wondered if this girl, Joe Ann, was also named after her daddy.

When she entered the room, Reverend Jenkins rushed over to her and embraced her, patting her gently on the back. Then he held her at arm's length and said, "Child, I haven't seen you since you were the size of a gnat!"

"Me?" Joe Ann said with a giggle. She pointed at Hallelujah. "What about him? The last time I saw this little fellow, he was running around in church shouting, 'Hallelujah! Hallelujah! Hallelujah!'"

We all laughed at the reminder of how my friend got his nickname.

"Look at you," Reverend Jenkins said. "I can't believe how quickly you grew up. Where were you when we came by last Saturday?"

Joe Ann's forehead creased. "Miss Bertha didn't tell you?" she asked. "I'm in college now."

Reverend Jenkins's eyebrows shot up. "College? Already? At sixteen?"

Joe Ann nodded. "Yes, sir. I started at Tougaloo back in September."

"Like your mother, huh?" said Reverend Jenkins.

"Yes," Joe Ann answered. "Except she skipped first and sixth grades, and I skipped first and fifth."

When Joe Ann spoke, her face seemed to smile, even without the aid of upturned lips. I couldn't believe she was in college. At sixteen. And there was poor Queen at sixteen about to have to drop out of high school.

She also seemed quite sophisticated, like Ophelia the Ogre from Saint Louis. But I bet she wouldn't make someone walk out to the toilet in the middle of the summer heat just to ridicule them the way Ophelia had done me back in August.

"Would y'all like some RCs?" Joe Ann asked. "Or I could fix some coffee if y'all think it's too cold for cola."

RC? Royal Crown cola? I had seen folks drink it, but I had never tasted it myself. Hallelujah had even seen in a newspaper where a Negro baseball player named Junior Gilliam, who played for some team called the Dodgers, claimed RC was his favorite cola. Before I had time to think about it, I blurted out, "I'd like a cola."

Joe Ann snapped her attention my way. She stared at me as if just noticing I was even in the room.

"Oh," was all she said.

The moment was awkward, to say the least.

"I'll have some coffee if it's not too much trouble," said Reverend Jenkins.

Hallelujah smiled my way and said, "I'll take a cola, too."

Miss Bertha appeared in the doorway and said to Joe Ann, "Your mama wants you." To Reverend Jenkins she said, "I'm going to finish gathering my things." She hurried out of the doorway before he could protest.

"Mama," Joe Ann called as she followed Miss Bertha from the room. "Guess who's here?"

"I know Clyde's here, Joe Ann," her mama called back.

"Hallelujah, too," said Joe Ann, her voice flowing throughout the house. "And they brought a cute little girl with them."

Hallelujah glanced at me and blushed. I guess we were both thinking the same thing. Joe Ann thought I was his girl-friend. Now I was doubly embarrassed.

"What's her name?" I heard the mama ask. Joe Ann hur-ried back to the room and poked her head in the doorway.

"What's your name?" she asked me.

"Rosa," I replied.

Joe Ann disappeared from the doorway yelling, "Mamaaa, she said her name is Rosa."

"Oh, that's pretty," came the reply.

This time Hallelujah smiled at me and said, "I told you, 'A pretty name for a pretty girl.'"

I wanted to take one of those floral-print pillows from the sofa and toss it at him. Instead I only smiled.

The moment the nutty aroma of coffee filled the air, Reverend Jenkins joined Miss Bertha and Joe Ann's mama in the kitchen. When Joe Ann returned with colas for Hallelujah and me, I was strolling around the room admiring their fam-ily photos.

"They're gorgeous, aren't they?" Joe Ann asked.

At first I thought she was being cocky, like Ophelia the Ogre. But then she added, "My daddy takes great photos. He's a professional photographer."

"You have a beautiful family," I said.

Joe Ann smiled and said, "We'll do. I guess."

"Is this your daddy?" I asked, pointing to a man in a soldier's uniform.

"Yes. He fought in the Second World War." Then she pointed at a picture of a young white woman, elegantly dressed, holding a bouquet of flowers. "And that's my mama."

I startled. And my mouth was still hanging open when Joe Ann added, "She's colored, not white."

Noticing the awkwardness, Hallelujah quickly changed the subject. "Is Mr. Thomas at his studio today?"

Joe Ann rolled her eyes. "He's *always* there on Saturday. You know it's the only day of the week when folks want their pictures taken."

My heart warmed as I imagined what it would be like to be a part of a family like Joe Ann's. Perhaps someday I could have a family like that of my own.

The RC colas were great, and so was Joe Ann's company. While the grownups chatted in the kitchen, she regaled Hallelujah and me with stories about her first semester in college.

She told us about when she first arrived at Tougaloo and how scared she was because she was only sixteen, and the other freshmen were eighteen, nineteen, and even twenty. She told us how she felt intimated because she was from the Delta, until she realized that students came from all parts of the state. Some of them were even children of sharecroppers, she said.

This gave me hope. Sitting and listening to Joe Ann talk about Tougaloo reminded me of something Miss Johnson had said. She said one of her cousins had attended Alcorn College only because her father wouldn't allow her to attend Tougaloo. He said Tougaloo didn't welcome dark-skinned Negroes, like her cousin. Yet, there I was, listening to a girl with very dark skin speak of her adventures at the college. It's like Papa always said: "Believe little of what you hear and only half of what you see."

I wanted to stay in Joe Ann's presence forever. I wanted to be a part of her family. As I sat there wishing she was my older sister, a shrill sound rocked me from my daydreaming. I had heard that sound only one other time in my life— while helping Ma Pearl at the Robinsons. It was a telephone. I would be forever amazed that through a little black object connected to the wall with a cord, people could talk to one another from all the way on the other side of the country. Perhaps one day—after I had gone to college and gotten a good job—I would buy such an item for Papa, so I could talk to him from wherever I chose to live.

"I got it, Mama," Joe Ann called.

The phone was in the hallway. And when Joe Ann left to answer it, Hallelujah turned to me and said, "I'm gonna work a little harder so I can finish high school early and go to college."

"She seems so grown-up," I said. "I can't believe she's only sixteen."

Hallelujah laughed. "Sixteen going on sixty, as your grandpa would say."

"Mr. Jenkins, it's for you!" we heard Joe Ann call from the hallway.

"Why would your daddy get a call here?" I asked Hallelujah.

He shrugged. "He never leaves Stillwater without letting at least two people know where he's going, in case someone needs to get in touch with him. Or in case something happens to him on the road, especially with the way things are now."

It seemed less than a minute passed from the time we heard Joe Ann inform Reverend Jenkins of his telephone call and the scream that came from the kitchen.

"Lord, no!" Joe Ann's mama screamed.

Chapter Nineteen

SATURDAY, DECEMBER 3

WHEN REVEREND JENKINS ENTERED THE ROOM, HE had the same look on his face as the day he announced the shooting of Gus Courts. Before he said a word, I knew it had happened again. Another Negro in Mississippi had been shot.

"We need to head over to Glendora," Reverend Jenkins said to Hallelujah. Then he stared at me, as if he faced a dilemma. "We need to get you home first."

"What's wrong?" Hallelujah asked.

"There's been a shooting in Glendora. A service station attendant. They say he was shot by one of J. W. Milam's friends. It was Milam's car he was driving."

Hallelujah and I sucked in air at the same time. "Milam!" he cried. "He just got away with killing Emmett Till!"

Fear rushed to my bones. I felt so cold, it seemed my blood stopped flowing. "They just shot Gus Courts," I said quietly. "Two shootings. Only a week apart."

It's a good thing I was sitting, else I would have crumpled to the floor. Someone who was a friend of J. W. Milam had just shot another Negro. Did he think it was okay to shoot a Negro because Milam got away with murder? Or had whites in the Delta simply gone mad?

Reverend Jenkins slumped in a chair. Hallelujah rushed to him and placed his arm around his shoulders. When he dropped his face into his palms, I prayed he wouldn't cry again.

With his head swaying from side to side, he half spoke, half moaned. "The killing has got to stop."

Hallelujah's voice was hoarse when he spoke. "What happened this time?"

What happened *this time?* The words bounced around in my head. The killing of Negroes had become so common that "this time" was now part of the conversation, as if to indicate there would be a "next time."

"Clinton Melton," said Reverend Jenkins. "His name was Clinton Melton. He pumped gas in the man's car. There was some kind of mix-up in the amount he pumped and the amount the man requested. The man became enraged and threatened to get his shotgun and come back and shoot Clinton. Which is exactly what he did. In full view of many witnesses. Including the white gas station owner."

Slowly, Hallelujah removed his arm from around Reverend Jenkins's shoulders and stuffed his hands into his pants pockets. He stormed over to the wall and dropped his face forward into it. His moan was so long and anguished that I realized he'd stuffed his hands into his pockets to keep from banging the wall.

I, too, wanted to bang on something. Another Negro in Mississippi had been shot and killed by a white person in broad daylight. Again there were witnesses. Again there would probably be no punishment.

As scared as I was about Shorty's idea of violence for violence, I was beginning to feel that white folks might stop their reign of terror if they knew what it felt like to be the victim of terror themselves.

When Miss Bertha came into the room and announced that she was ready, Reverend Jenkins glared at her and said, "You're not going. You're staying here. Where it's safe."

Miss Bertha frowned and planted her hands on her hips. "Those people don't scare me."

Well, they scared me. And I would've given anything to trade places with Miss Bertha. I would have gladly stayed in Mound Bayou, at Joe Ann's house, in her stead.

"I'm tired of letting them push us around," Miss Bertha said. "I own a store. And I intend to run it. Besides, where are our people shopping in my absence?" She raised an eyebrow and said, "Danny Ray Martin's? You know how he likes to cheat the old folks."

Reverend Jenkins threw up his hands. "Clinton Melton was shot for no reason, Bertha. He wasn't involved with the NAACP. He wasn't rounding up people to register to vote. He didn't even make an advance toward one of their precious women, for God's sake. He was killed because his killer knew he could get away with it, just like his friend J. W. Milam got away with murder.

"Gus Courts was shot and almost killed because his killer knew he could get away with it, just like Reverend Lee's and Lamar Smith's killers got away with it. No one is going to do a darned thing about the slaughtering of Negroes in Mississippi. And if something happens to you, I swear upon my father's grave that I will take the law into my own hands."

I flinched.

Even Reverend Jenkins considered returning violence for violence if something happened to his family. How *could* people like Papa keep claiming to have peace at a time like this? If nothing else, like Shorty said, we needed to be armed and ready to protect our own.

Miss Bertha stared Reverend Jenkins straight in the eyes and said, "'The Spirit of the Lord is upon me, because he hath anointed me to preach the gospel to the poor; he hath sent me to heal the brokenhearted, to preach deliverance to the captives, and recovering of sight to the blind, to set at liberty them that are bruised.' Aren't those the words we live by, Clyde? Are they not the words our father left with us before he died?"

"You're not a preacher," Reverend Jenkins said.

"But the Lord has anointed me to serve the poor and brokenhearted, just as he anointed you," replied Miss Bertha.

Reverend Jenkins shook his head. "Sis," he pleaded. "Look at what an angry white man just did—shot a colored man right in front of a service station full of people, without the least bit of concern about the law. You know why?"

Miss Bertha, of course, didn't answer, as she knew the question was what Miss Johnson would call rhetorical.

"Because there is no law in Mississippi that protects Negroes from being killed. We have laws that protect wild animals, but none that protect a colored person.

"You're safe here," Reverend Jenkins said. "White folks won't come here starting trouble. They know better."

Miss Bertha shook her head. "I'm not some wild game that these people can hunt. I won't hide like a scared rabbit." She stared at Hallelujah. "Put my things in the trunk," she said. "I'm going home."

Chapter Twenty

SUNDAY, DECEMBER 4

FROM THE DOORWAY OF OUR BEDROOM, MA PEARL cried, "Rise and shine, saints!"

Church was the last place I wanted to be that morning. I was tired of church. Tired of trying to be good. Tired of listening to Reverend Jenkins compare the Israelites to Negroes. Tired of hearing him talk about how God delivered them from Pharaoh and led them to the Promise Land. Tired of hearing him talk about how if God did it before, he could do it again. Jesus Christ, the same yesterday, today, and forever. The Negro would soon see deliverance. The Negro wasn't seeing anything but bullets soaring toward them.

I had fallen asleep trembling the night before, thinking about that man Clinton Melton. He did nothing to whoever shot him. He wasn't trying to change things in the South. He wasn't one of those brave Negroes, walking through the valley of the shadow of death. Or maybe he was. Maybe just living in the South was like walking through that valley. Shorty was right. In Mississippi you never knew what could get you killed.

Clinton Melton had done nothing but pump gas into the man's car. So what if he heard him wrong and didn't pump the right amount? Was that a reason to kill him? But he didn't need a reason. He was one of J. W. Milam's friends, actually one of his workers, according to what Reverend Jenkins later found out. And if his boss man could get away with kidnapping, beating, and shooting a fourteen-year-old colored boy, then why couldn't he get away with shooting one for pumping too much gas into his tank?

"Rose Lee! Git up, gal! You too, Queen! Ain't none o' y'all sleepin' in this moan'n. Every last one o' ya gittin' outta here t'day."

I moaned but didn't move. Let her get her black strap. I didn't care. She could beat me until I turned blue, but I wasn't setting foot in another church. Jesus wasn't doing a thing to protect colored people in Mississippi, so I wasn't thinking about going to his house and worshiping him, his Father, nor their Holy Ghost.

Queen stirred. Then she sighed and said, "Ma Pearl, I'm too sick."

"Gal, you five months. You ain't got no moan'n sickness. Git up!"

Queen began to weep.

Ma Pearl stormed into the room and snatched the covers off her bed. "Git up 'fo I beat the devil outta you."

She turned and did the same to my bed, giving me the same warning.

I complied by sitting up on the side of the bed.

Queen curled into a ball and wept harder. "Ma Pearl, I'm too 'shamed to go to church."

"You shoulda thought o' that 'fo you went and got yo'self in trouble. Now git up."

Queen buried her face in her pillow and yelled, "I ain't goin'. I ain't never goin' to church again. And I ain't goin' back to school."

Ma Pearl stormed from the room.

"Queen, please," I said. "Just get up. Don't make her use that strap on you." Even though I initially thought I was bold enough to take it, I didn't want it again after the beating I got because of meeting Shorty Cooper, nor did I want a repeat of the beating Ma Pearl had given Queen the night she caught her sneaking out. Ma Pearl could be ruthless with that strap. As horrible as it was that Queen was in trouble, I didn't want to see any harm come to her or the baby she was carrying.

"I'm so sick of her!" Queen yelled. "She ain't nothin' but a bully. A big, tall, ugly bully. And I hate her. And I hate Papa for lettin' her treat us like this."

"Us?" I asked, pointing at myself. "Before you got in trouble, she used to treat you exactly like the name she gave you

—Queen. I'm the one she always treated like I was no better than hog slop."

Queen snorted, as if to say, "You ain't."

"Well, do what you want to," I said, leaping off the bed. "But I'm not getting a beating on a Sunday morning."

I might have been mad at Jesus for letting colored folks get killed in Mississippi, and I knew I stood a chance of a fire-and-brimstone damnation for my blasphemy. But at the moment it was Ma Pearl who was a threat with flesh and bones. So I chose sulking at church over a beating *and* sulking at church.

"Hand me them covers," Queen said.

"Get 'em yourself," I said.

She groaned, then reached down and pulled her covers off the floor. She wrapped herself in them and snuggled into a ball. "She don't wanna hurt my pretty baby," she said smugly. "So she ain't go'n beat me."

I rolled my eyes and said, "She already did."

Chapter Twenty-One

MONDAY, DECEMBER 5

Just as she had done with church, Queen refused to get up for school. She had dropped out.

Thankfully, Uncle Ollie was kind enough to continue giving Fred Lee and me a ride whether his stepdaughter—the queen—attended school or not. Otherwise, we would have faced the predicament of many other colored children. We would have had to walk the eight miles to and from school.

I expected Hallelujah to be waiting for me outside Miss Hill's classroom like he always was. Instead, he was inside the classroom. And from the noise flowing into the hallway, it seemed he had started another ruckus.

I walked in to find Hallelujah and two other eighth grade students, Barbara and her cousin Dorothy—the two who had defended him after he left Miss Hill's class—sitting atop the desks, their faces wild with excitement. Hallelujah was talking loudly and waving his arms wildly. When he saw me enter the room, he leaped up from the desk and rushed toward me.

He grabbed my wrists, causing the strap of my book satchel to slide down my arm.

"Rosa! It's happening!" he said.

"What's happening?" I asked. I glanced from face to face.

"Dr. Howard did it!" Hallelujah exclaimed, his face glowing. "He incited the people to take a stand."

"Can I at least sit down?" I said, annoyed.

I didn't know what people he was talking about, nor did I care. I didn't want to hear anything else about Dr. Howard or his speeches. Dr. Howard and his speeches weren't keeping Negroes from getting shot in Mississippi.

Hallelujah stared at his hands gripping my wrists. "Oh, sorry," he said, releasing his grip. But he beamed again and said, "I'm just so excited." Grinning, he sat in the desk next to mine.

I glanced from face to smiling face. "So what's all this commotion about?" I asked.

Barbara and Dorothy leaned in as Hallelujah recounted to me what he had obviously already told them: Colored people in Montgomery, Alabama, were about to start a bus boycott, and it was all because of a colored lady who got arrested for not giving up her seat so that a white person could sit down.

Hallelujah stared wild-eyed at me and gripped my wrists again. "You're not gonna believe this!" he said. "The lady who refused to give up her seat is named Rosa—just like you!"

Barbara and Dorothy clapped and cheered as if I had done something. Some colored lady with the same name as me had been arrested because she wouldn't stand up and let a white man have her seat, and they were cheering for me?

I wriggled my wrists from Hallelujah's grasp. "Okay, let me get this straight," I said. "Dr. Howard gave his big speech in Montgomery, Alabama, a week ago Saturday, right?"

Hallelujah nodded eagerly.

"Then on Thursday a colored lady named Rosa wouldn't stand up to let a white person sit down. And today colored folks aren't supposed to ride the buses because she got arrested?"

"Yep, that's right," Hallelujah said.

"But why are y'all cheering for me?"

"Remember what you told me about your name coming from some saint from Italy?

"Rose of Viterbo," I said. "It means 'dew.'"

"Like the stuff on the grass in the mornings?" asked Dorothy.

Before I could answer, Hallelujah chimed in. "She says people with this name want to analyze and understand the world. They search for deep truths."

I shook my head at them all as they stared at me. "I still don't understand how this has anything to do with me."

Dorothy shrugged. "Well, it don't, really. But we just excited to have a Rosa among us, seeing that this Rosa lady just stood up to a white man."

Hallelujah laughed and said, "Or shall we say, 'She *wouldn't* stand up *for* a white man'?"

While my classmates laughed with Hallelujah, I pondered how, until that very day, neither of them had bothered calling me Rosa. Like with Ma Pearl and everyone else, I was just Rose Lee to them.

"I still don't understand the whole bus thing," I said.

Barbara nudged Hallelujah. "Explain it to her, like you told us."

Hallelujah rose and took his preacher's stance. "The city buses in Montgomery," he said, "have two sections—one for whites, up front, of course, and one for coloreds, in the back. But if the white section is full, then colored folks have to get up and allow the white people to have their seats. But Mrs. Rosa Parks said she was tired of giving in to white folks. So when the bus driver asked her to let a white person have her seat, she said no—"

"And she got arrested and put in jail," interrupted Dorothy.

"So what's this about a boycott?" I asked.

Hallelujah pulled a piece of paper from his pants pocket. "How could I forget to show you this?" He unfolded the paper and handed it to me. "Preacher said this is classified information. It's part of a letter an NAACP worker named Jo Ann Robinson distributed throughout the colored sections in Montgomery on Saturday. I copied down the important parts."

"Robinson?" I asked, my brows raised. "She colored?"

"I just told you she's NAACP," Hallelujah answered. "Of course she's colored."

"'Another Negro woman has been arrested and thrown in jail because she refused to get up out of her seat on the bus and give it to a white person,'" I read aloud. "'This has to be stopped. We are, therefore, asking every Negro to stay off the buses Monday in protest of the arrest and trial. Don't ride the buses to work, to town, to school, or anywhere on Monday.'"

I glanced up at Hallelujah. "It says *another* Negro woman. It's happened before?"

"Yeah," answered Hallelujah. "Preacher said it happened earlier this year. Two others, he thinks, got arrested for not giving up their seats. It says another Negro woman, but I think one of them was about our age."

"Oh," I said, thinking about Joe Ann in Mound Bayou. She'd probably be the type of Negro who would be that brave.

Joe Ann and Hallelujah, of course. I studied the note again before handing it back to him. "So how do you know it's a boycott? How do you know it's not just for one day?"

Barbara nudged him again. "Tell her 'bout the meeting."

"They're having a meeting tonight at the church where Dr. Howard held his rally. Dexter Avenue. The one where that young preacher, Reverend Martin Luther King, pastors. Preacher says they're holding a meeting tonight to strategize how to keep this going. To make it a real boycott. But for today they're asking every colored person to stay off the buses."

Barbara chimed in. "It don't matter if it's one day or one hundred days. What's important is that they do it."

"And how do they know colored people will stay off the buses like they asked?" I said.

Hallelujah glanced at the note again. "Preacher said he was sure they would." He folded the note and stuffed it into his pocket. "He said folks are sick and tired of being sick and tired."

"He got that right." Shorty's voice boomed from the doorway. "I'm sho' sick and ti'ed."

"Shorty!" I gasped. I was so glad to see him that I almost leaped from my seat to run and hug him. I was so glad that he wasn't in jail. Or dead.

Chapter Twenty-Two

MONDAY, DECEMBER 5

Dorothy frowned and said, "Where you been all this time, Shorty Cooper? You ain't been to school in two weeks."

Shorty answered flatly, "Mindin' my bizness. Leavin' yours 'lone."

"How you jest go'n show up all of a sudden and stick yo' nose up in this conversation?" Barbara asked.

Shorty ignored both Dorothy and Barbara and turned to Hallelujah. "How is a few Negroes not ridin' the bus in Alabama go'n keep Negroes in Miss'sippi from gittin' shot?" He folded his arms over his chest and said, "A white man jest walked up to a colored man on Saturday 'n shot him over some gasoline. And y'all up in here clappin' 'cause a colored woman was too ti'ed to git out of a seat."

Hallelujah glowered at him and said, "You don't know anything, James Cooper."

Shorty glowered back at him. "You thank you and yo' daddy the only somebody that know what's goin' on 'round here? That doctor in Mound Bayou sayin' one thang to the press, and another to the peoples. He tellin' the press that there go'n be bloodshed in Miss'sippi. That both black and white blood go'n be runnin' in the streets if Eisenhower don't do nothin' 'bout this killin'. But he tellin' the peoples to march in the streets. Which is it go'n be, Preacha'? Marchin' or shootin'?"

Hallelujah glared up and down at Shorty. "Guess you think we should all do like you and sneak around at night and shoot at white folks' houses, huh?"

"What?" Barbara asked, her eyes widening.

Shorty cut his eyes at her. "They doin' a heck of a lot worse to us. And I don't need no *Jet* magazine to tell me 'bout it. I was there this time. I seen it for myself.

"That peckerwood, Elmer Kimball, drove up to the station. Ast for a fill-up. McGarrh, the boss man, told Melton to fill up the tank. After he fill't it up, that peckerwood started cussin' 'n screamin' that he didn't ast for no fill-up. But we all heard him say, 'Fill 'er up.' He lied like a sack o' rocks and said he only ast for a dollar worth in his tank."

Barbara interrupted Shorty. "You was there *f'real*?"

"I was there. Right outside the sto' 'cause my truck wouldn't start. That's where I been all this time. Up in Glendora, working. My granmama's brother got me a job doing some carpentry work. Stopped by that station for some gas, then my truck quit. I seen everythang."

"You saw the whole thing?" Dorothy asked.

Shorty nodded. "The whole thang."

Hallelujah rolled his eyes.

"When that fool said he was go'n to git his shotgun, the boss man McGarrh told Melton to hurr'up 'n git home." Shorty shook his head and said, "Melton's car was outta gas. 'Fo he could fill it up, Kimball was back."

"Lordy," Dorothy whispered.

"And he just shot him?" Barbara asked.

"In cold blood," said Shorty. "Went afta him like he was out 'n the woods huntin' a deer or somethin'."

"Open season on the Negro," I said quietly, glancing at Hallelujah.

He said nothing.

Shorty shook his head. "The white man that own the service station begged that man not to shoot. Told him what a good man Melton was. 'A hard-working Negro with a family,' he said."

When Dorothy moaned, Shorty shook his head again and said, "He begged him not to shoot."

"But he shot him anyways," Barbara said quietly. She dropped her head, wrapped her arms around her stomach, and muttered, "Umph, umph, umph."

Shorty glared at Hallelujah and said, "So I ast you again, Preacha', how is a few Negroes not ridin' the bus in Alabama go'n keep Negroes in Miss'sippi from gittin' shot? If that doctor in Mound Bayou really cared, he'a be here in Miss'sippi doin' somethin' 'bout the killin's 'stead o' runnin' over to Alabama jest shoutin' 'bout 'em."

Hallelujah gave Shorty a harsh up-and-down look. He stared at him hard for a moment without speaking. "So you were there. You saw a killing. And all of a sudden you think that makes you more dedicated than Dr. T. R. M. Howard? What did you do when Emmett Till was murdered?"

There was no reply from Shorty.

"Did you host all those people from the North in your home during the trial? Did you protect Emmett Till's mother when she was worried about what these white folks down here might do to her? Did you spearhead an all-out search for the colored folks who witnessed the crime?"

He glared at Shorty and waited for a response.

When there wasn't one, Hallelujah continued. "Are you traveling from city to city demanding that something be done about these killings? Or are you just hell-bent on picking up your shotgun and doing what that peckerwood just did up in Glendora?"

Hallelujah stared Shorty square in the face and said, "Buckshot don't discriminate. Remember that before you consider firing your shotgun."

For what felt like the longest seconds in history, Shorty

simply stared right back at Hallelujah. And within those seconds, a darkness seemed to creep into the room.

When Shorty finally spoke, his voice was calmer than I expected, considering the anger in his eyes. "You know what the rest of us was doin' while Kimball was firin' that shotgun, Preacha'?" He shook his head. "Nah. You don't. 'Cause you wasn't there. You ain't never been there. Yo' doctor in Mound Bayou ain't never been there." He stepped closer to Hallelujah and said, "Well, Preacha', let me tell you what we was doin'. We was all hidin' in the station. Every last one of us. You know how come? 'Cause Kimball woulda been happy to hit any one of us that day.

"So you tell me. Which one go'n work? Boycotts or bullets?"

Before Hallelujah could reply, Miss Hill entered the classroom. She took one look at Hallelujah, scowled, then said, "I know all about that mess going on in Alabama, and I certainly don't need to deal with that kind of nonsense in my classroom this morning." She pointed at the door and said, "Leave. Right. Now."

Chapter Twenty-Three

MONDAY, DECEMBER 5

I SAT ON THE PORCH TO WORK MATH PROBLEMS BE-cause little Abigail was making too much noise inside the house for me to concentrate. It's too bad she wasn't old enough to fear Ma Pearl like the rest of Aunt Ruthie's children. Ear infection or any other pain, they would somehow figure out a way to suppress their cries in her presence.

But it wasn't just Abigail who hindered my ability to concentrate. It was everything around me. I stared at the nearly leafless oak in our front yard. Its winding roots making their way toward the front porch reminded me of snakes. I imagined those snakes having the faces of people like Roy Bryant, J. W. Milam, Elmer Kimball, Ricky Turner, and even the lady who had hissed "niggers" at Mrs. Robinson's Cackling Church Club meeting. The ancient oak was their precious way of life, and they were ready to strike, with their venom, anyone who dared come near it.

While a potential bus boycott in Montgomery was a good thing, I could understand Shorty's anger and wanting to do something more to protect ourselves. But even if Clinton Melton had had a gun, what could he have done? Would he have shot a white man who was threatening to shoot him first? And if he had, what would be his punishment?

If he had been able to leave the service station and head home before Elmer Kimball got back with his shotgun, would Elmer Kimball, Roy Bryant, and J. W. Milam have gone to his house in the middle of the night and "taken him" like they had done Emmett Till?

Sometimes when Papa faced a tough decision, he would shake his head and say that he was trapped between a rock and a hard spot. And that's where the Negro was. There was probably nothing Clinton Melton could have done that day to save his life. Nothing. Because Elmer Kimball probably got up that morning with an urge to kill a Negro.

When Miss Hill ordered Hallelujah to leave her classroom that morning, Shorty had stormed out too, with fire in his eyes. No one had seen him the rest of the day. I prayed he hadn't, like my cousin Mule in Arkansas, gone out and done something foolish.

I knew Shorty wasn't the sharpest thorn on the bush when it came to school, but so much of what he said made sense. How was a bus boycott in Montgomery, Alabama, going to keep colored people in Mississippi from getting slaughtered like hogs? It was almost as if the only way to survive was to leave. But I had already passed up that opportunity.

The squeaking screen door jolted me from my thoughts. When Aunt Ruthie stepped out, her face said she needed some peace. Worry lines creased her forehead, and redness blurred her eyes. With a sigh, she dropped onto the chair next to mine and flayed her arms and legs. It was unladylike, but she sure looked comfortable.

She let her head fall back and let out another long, tired sigh. She swept a curl from her sweaty face and shut her eyes. "Rose," she whispered, "don't have chi'ren 'less you got a good husband to help you take care of 'em."

I was about to respond until I saw the tear roll from the side of Aunt Ruthie's eye.

I placed my math book, paper, and pencil on the porch floor and took Aunt Ruthie's hand into mine. Neither of us said a word as we listened to the sounds of nature and allowed them to soothe us.

Five children, all seven years old and under, and Aunt Ruthie had to care for them the whole day in addition to helping Ma Pearl out around the house. It was too bad Lil' John and Virgil still hadn't started school even though they were already seven and six years old. There was no way to get them there, and it was too far for them to walk. Even with Queen out of school, they still couldn't catch a ride with Uncle Ollie. With Aunt Clara Jean's three other children being in school, the car was already overpacked before Queen's absence.

After talking with Hallelujah about that whole bus thing in Montgomery, Alabama, I thought about how wonderful it would be to have a bus to ride to school like the white children. Some places in Mississippi, according to Hallelujah, had begun supplying buses for the colored children to ride, but Stillwater wasn't one of those places. He also said the schoolchildren in big cities like Montgomery, and even our very own Jackson, Mississippi, could ride the city bus to school if they had the means to pay the fare. Of course, that probably wouldn't have done Aunt Ruthie's children any good. Aunt Ruthie didn't have money to buy food, so where would she get money to pay for her children to ride a bus to school?

She taught them at home as best she could. But with her own education lacking, I didn't know how much she was able to teach her children. I did my best to pick up the slack when I came home, but I had my own catching up to do, seeing I had missed two months of school myself.

I stared at Aunt Ruthie—weary and worn from a bad marriage and the burden of caring for her small children all by herself—and wondered whether staying in Mississippi would put me at risk of turning out like her. Why didn't she have the grit to defy Ma Pearl like Aunt Belle had? She had been offered the opportunity to go to Saint Louis, but Ma Pearl wouldn't allow her. So she settled, marrying the first thing that came her way. Now she had returned—sad and broken—to the place she had so desperately wanted to escape.

I tried to imagine Aunt Ruthie living up north. During the summer she would visit the South like the other northern Negroes. She would pull into the yard in a big black car. I imagined her honking the horn with one hand and waving out the window with the other. She would be wearing a wide-brimmed fancy white hat. And the grin stretched across her face would reveal her pearly white teeth. She would always wear a smile, because she would be happy.

And when she married, it would be to a good man. A decent man. A man who worked—all the time, and not just when he felt like it. A man who didn't drink spirits, as Papa called them. Spirits that controlled his mind and told him it was okay to hit his wife and curse his children.

But I also imagined Aunt Ruthie being happy where she was. Maybe there was still a way.

"Aunt Ruthie," I said, with a slight squeeze of her hand. "It's not too late."

Aunt Ruthie sat up in her chair and, with the back of her

free hand, wiped the tears from her face. "Not too late for what?" she asked, her voice raspy.

"It's not too late to be what you wanted to be," I said.

Aunt Ruthie shook her head. "I don't know what I ever wanted to be. Other than outta this house." She motioned toward the parlor door and said, "Now I'm back."

Aunt Ruthie had an education, even if it wasn't the best. Aunt Belle only had an eighth-grade education, but she still ended up opening her own beauty shop. She used her talents to find her own way, and so could Aunt Ruthie. She was a great cook. She was also good at doing hair. And Lord knows she knew how to take care of children.

"You ever thought about baking cakes and selling them?" I asked.

"Where I'm go'n git the money to buy the stuff to bake the cakes?" she asked.

I gestured toward the house. "We have plenty of flour and sugar and everything else you need to make pound cakes. And everybody knows you make the best pound cake in town."

Aunt Ruthie shook her head. "That ain't my kitchen. And that ain't my stuff."

"Papa wouldn't mind you using what we have to make cakes and sell 'em."

Aunt Ruthie's face tightened. "But Mama would. If I used

her flour and sugar and baked cakes in her kitchen, she take every penny I made from sellin' 'em and keep for her own."

That wrenched my heart because it was true. I thought about Shorty, and what he said about my daddy, Johnny Lee Banks. Johnny Lee gave him and his grandparents money to help them out. I wished there was some way I could get in touch with him, then maybe he could help us out. Maybe I could ask him for a small amount of money and give it to Aunt Ruthie to buy her own supplies.

When I told Aunt Ruthie about my idea, she shook her head and said it wouldn't work. "She ain't go'n let me use her kitchen nohow. Not to make money that she cain't keep."

"She can keep some of it," I said. "Even slave owners did that much." I told her about what Reverend Jenkins had said about Joseph Davis allowing his slaves to work outside his plantation, and how he allowed them to keep the money.

"They only paid him for the time spent off his plantation," I said.

Aunt Ruthie squinted at me and said, "Chile, yo' granmama worse than a slave owner."

"No one is worse than a slave owner," I said.

"Well, she as greedy as one," countered Aunt Ruthie.

We both chuckled even though the subject was serious.

"I think you should at least try," I said.

Aunt Ruthie pursed her lips. "How we s'pose explain

where I'm gittin' money to buy the flour and sugar and vanilla flavor? And you know she go'n charge me extra for using her butter and eggs and milk."

When I creased my forehead in thought, Aunt Ruthie said, "And even if you could git money from yo' daddy, you sho' cain't tell her you gittin' money from him. Lawd knows she despise that man. And as greedy as she is, she still ain't go'n be happy 'bout you takin' money from him."

"You can say you got it from Slow John," I suggested.

Aunt Ruthie chortled. "Now we all know hell'a freeze over 'fo that happen."

"Oh, I know," I said. "What if we ask Miss Bertha to help us out? She might agree to saying she gave you the supplies on loan."

This time Aunt Ruthie's forehead creased. "Maybe we should jest do that anyway. Maybe Bertha'll jest let me have the supplies on credit, and you won't have to take nothin' from Johnny Lee."

"But how you gonna pay Ma Pearl up front?"

"If Miss Bertha can wait to git paid, then Mama can too."

My face lit up. "So you're gonna do it?"

Aunt Ruthie smiled and nodded. "Sho' is. And with Christmas comin' up, I can probably git a lotta sales."

By this time, I was beaming so hard I felt my face would explode. I was so happy for Aunt Ruthie and the possibility that she would be at least trying to do something to help her and her children. Maybe then Ma Pearl wouldn't be so grumpy toward her. Then a thought hit me.

"I don't understand Ma Pearl," I said. "As greedy as she is, why wouldn't she let us take money from my daddy? Does she hate him that much for getting Mama in trouble? Seems to me she'd want him to pay her restitution for ruining her daughter."

Aunt Ruthie laughed and said, "That ain't the only reason." She held out her hand and showed me the backside of it. I observed its smooth darkness.

"Because he's *dark*?" I asked.

"Chile, Mama thank darkness is a curse. The dark Negroes worked in the fields. The yellow ones worked in the house. She thank the lighter you is, the better off you is. She ain't got no kinda love for black folks." Aunt Ruthie rolled her eyes and said, "Humph. She thank I'm the biggest curse of all."

"How come?"

"She ain't dark. Papa ain't dark. But I'm black as the ace of spades. Now, how that happen 'less I'm some kinda curse God sent her for hatin' her own skin?"

"Aunt Ruthie, don't talk like that," I said.

Aunt Ruthie frowned. "Rose, it's the truth. Aunt Isabelle

said Mama wouldn't even hold me after she birthed me. She told Miss Addie she could take me out to the woods and leave me there for bears to raise for all she cared."

"Then how come she didn't let you go to Saint Louis with Great-Aunt Isabelle if she hates you so much?"

"It's 'cause she hate me."

"I don't understand," I said.

"When you hate somebody, you don't want nothin' good for 'em, even if they yo' own flesh 'n blood. She didn't want me to go up there and make somethin' outta myself. She wanted me stuck here."

"That why didn't she let you marry Reverend Jenkins?"

A smile spread across Aunt Ruthie's face. "How you know 'bout that?"

"Hallelujah told me," I said, smiling back.

"She wadn't go'n let me marry no preacher. She didn't thank I was good 'nuff for no preacher."

"So you married Slow John," I said quietly.

Aunt Ruthie shook her head. "He wadn't always like that. He wadn't drankin' that much when I marr'd him. He took to hittin' the bottle real hard when Mr. Robinson thowed us off his place."

That wasn't the way I'd heard the story, but I didn't say that to Aunt Ruthie. "Well, he's gone now," I said. "And you can have a fresh start. You can get to baking those cakes and selling them. And who knows where that could lead to next."

"Humph," Aunt Ruthie said, half smiling, half smirking. "That's if Mama let me."

"She'll let you," I said. "I'm gonna see if I can get on good speaking terms with Jesus again and pray about it."

Aunt Ruthie studied me for a moment, then smiled. "You sho' is growin' up, Miss Rose Lee Carter."

Something about Aunt Ruthie's words gave me goose bumps. As I wrapped my arms around myself and rubbed them away, I thought again about what was going on in Montgomery. Hallelujah had said the lady who would not give up her seat on the bus was named Rosa—like me. My classmates were celebrating the fact that someone named Rosa was among them. Could I grow up and be strong like this woman?

I told Aunt Ruthie about Mrs. Rosa Parks and what Monty said about our name.

She smiled broadly. "Well, if Miz Rosa Parks is anythang like Miss Rose—pardon me—Rosa Lee Carter, then she is one special lady."

Chapter Twenty-Four

TUESDAY, DECEMBER 6

THAT MORNING WHEN I SAW HALLELUJAH WAITING for me outside Miss Hill's class, his smile was brighter than a summer sun. I knew he had good news to share, but before he did I wanted to ask him about getting Miss Bertha to help out Aunt Ruthie.

"Yes, yes, yes," he said quickly after I informed him of the plan. "That's the whole reason she has the store, so she can help people. She'll be glad to give Miss Ruthie credit."

I was annoyed that he didn't seem as excited about Aunt Ruthie as I did. "Aren't you happy for her? This is her chance to make something of herself if everything goes as planned. The next thing we know she could own a bakery in town."

Hallelujah's spirit deflated. He pursed his lips and said, "I *am* happy for Miss Ruthie. I'm always happy when good things happen for our people. But what I need to tell you goes beyond just one person. It could impact the whole colored race."

I was still a bit disappointed that he didn't seem as excited about Aunt Ruthie's potential cake-selling business as I thought he would be, but I perked up and listened to what he had to share just the same.

Hallelujah's face lit up again. "So Preacher got word late last night that very few Negroes rode the city buses in Montgomery yesterday."

"How many usually ride?"

Hallelujah shrugged. "I don't know. With all the people going to work and the children going to school, hundreds, maybe, thousands." He grabbed my hand and said, "The point is, the boycott worked! Colored people stayed off the buses yesterday. And guess what?"

I was still having a hard time sharing his enthusiasm. I shook my hand from his grasp. "What?" I asked dryly.

"They're continuing the boycott. It won't be just a one-day thing."

"What about the children?" I asked. "How will they get to school?" I thought about Aunt Ruthie's children sitting at home, hopefully learning how to read and write. And count.

"The details haven't been worked out yet. But for now they're asking people to do what they did yesterday—to stay off the buses."

"And what will that do?"

"A boycott is a peaceful way to protest all this unfair treatment," Hallelujah answered. "Preacher said that sometimes colored folks pay their fares at the front of the bus, and by the time they walk around to the back where they have to enter, the driver will speed off. The boycott organizers said that if the city loses enough money from colored people not riding the buses, they'll make some changes."

I shrugged. "It's just a bus. What about all this other stuff? Like the schools and people getting killed for registering to vote?"

Hallelujah shook his head. "It's a start. And it's a peaceful start. The police can't arrest anyone for not riding a bus."

I thought of Mr. Robinson's warning to throw people off his place if they got involved with the NAACP. "Can't people lose their jobs?"

Hallelujah shrugged again. "As long as they show up, why should white folks care how their colored workers get there?"

I crossed my arms and glared at him. "You, of all people, should know that it's not about how colored people get to work but more about white folks making sure they keep their power. Separate, but unequal. Whites fighting to protect what they think belongs to their future generation. Negroes fighting to make life better for theirs."

Hallelujah smiled and raised his brows. "I'm impressed."

"You making fun of me?"

"No," he said, quickly. "I'm proud of you. I've never heard you say anything like that before."

I shrugged. "I think talking with Aunt Ruthie helped

me figure out how to express what I've always known in my heart."

I recounted to Hallelujah what Aunt Ruthie had said about Ma Pearl not allowing her to marry Reverend Jenkins or to go to Saint Louis and live with Great-Aunt Isabelle—how it all came down to Ma Pearl wanting less for her, because she didn't see any value in her life.

"It's a shame when our own people hold each other back," Hallelujah said. "I'll make sure I tell Aunt Bertha about Miss Ruthie's plan. Who knows? Maybe our aunts can go into business together. Maybe Aunt Bertha could sell your aunt's cakes in her store."

Before I could respond to Hallelujah, we were interrupted by a couple of ninth-graders who approached him with questions about the bus situation in Montgomery. Hallelujah was more than eager to share information with them.

"Maybe I'll see you at lunch," he said to me.

I smiled, nodded, then headed toward my own classroom. The bus boycott in Montgomery might have been on their minds, but Aunt Ruthie was on mine. If Miss Bertha gave her the items she needed to bake cakes on credit, and if Ma Pearl allowed her to use her kitchen to bake them, *and* if Miss Bertha sold Aunt Ruthie's cakes in her store, then that would basically make Aunt Ruthie a businesswoman like Aunt Belle. That would make her what Miss Johnson called an entrepreneur. And it would make me, her niece, very proud.

When the ninth-graders showed up for lunch, Hallelujah entered the lunchroom flanked by a group of mostly girls. His knowledge of the bus boycott in Montgomery had brought him up to a new level of popularity.

After he grabbed a tray from the very short line of students who could afford to buy lunch, he sat among his new friends and beckoned me over to their table. Feeling shy, I shook my head, lowered my gaze, and pretended to search for food in my already empty lunch sack.

But Hallelujah did not give up. "Rosa, come join us," he called out.

I glanced up to find his table mates staring at me. With a sigh, I grabbed my lunch sack and joined them. When Dorothy and Barbara from the eighth grade class saw me, they also got up and joined us. Now there were eight of us — five girls and three boys — at a table that seated six.

"So your name really is Rosa, like the lady in Alabama?" a light-skinned, freckled girl named Gertrude asked me when I squeezed onto the bench beside Hallelujah.

I smiled and answered, "Yes." And just as I was about to

explain what the name meant, Gertrude gave me a quick up-and-down glance, wrinkled up her nose, and said, "I always thought your name was just plain Rose."

She said it in a tone that indicated I wasn't worthy of the name.

"Rosa changed her name when she got baptized in October," Hallelujah explained.

I glared sideways at him and said, "I didn't change my name. Rosa is the name my mama gave me. It's on my birth certificate."

They all stared at me like I had swallowed a canary and suddenly turned yellow.

Clearing her throat, Dorothy broke the silence. "Her name is special. It means 'dew,' or something like that."

Gertrude gave her the same condescending stare that she had given me. After which she addressed Hallelujah: "So, what all do you know about the bus boycott?"

"Well, first of all," he said, smiling, "yesterday's one-day boycott was a success. So some of the leading Negroes in Montgomery formed themselves into a group called the Montgomery Improvement Association, or the MIA."

One of the boys, Edward, the one Shorty had asked to join his night riding gang, rubbed his hands together and said, "Oh, I like that. M-I-A. Like Missing in Action. Like ain't no Negroes on the bus today 'cause they all missing in action."

The group chuckled and nodded in agreement.

Hallelujah beamed. "And that young preacher I told y'all about? Reverend King?"

Around the table, heads bobbed.

"The MIA elected him as their leader," Hallelujah continued.

Dorothy interrupted. "See. That's what we need to do. We need to form us a group and select a leader."

"The Stillwater Improvement Association," suggested Barbara. "SIA."

Edward shook his head. "Nah. That don't have no kinda ring to it. No kinda significance."

Barbara crossed her arms and glared at him. "Then what do you suggest?"

After a roll of her eyes, Gertrude interjected. "I suggest we allow Jenkins to finish telling us about what's going on in Montgomery, *then* we can start worrying about forming a group and giving ourselves a name."

I don't know whether it was because Gertrude annoyed me or because some new wave of bravery had suddenly washed over me, but I looked her straight in her light brown eyes and said, "I like the idea of forming a group. It shows unity." I turned to Edward and said, "How 'bout the Negro Youth Council?"

Gertrude turned up her nose. "You mean like that ol' White Citizens' Council?"

"I like it," said Edward. "Negro Youth Council. See the letters? N-Y-C. Like we down here in Stillwater, Mississippi, marching like them folks up there in New York City. Yeah, I like it. Negro Youth Council. N-Y-C," he said again, his head bobbing.

Gertrude cut her eyes at him so hard that it's a wonder he wasn't sliced in two.

"So that mean you in, Rosa?" Barbara asked. "You go'n leave Robinson's place long enough to do something with us here in town?"

My stomach felt like it flipped upside down. I hadn't thought about actually *doing* something. I only wanted to show up Gertrude by suggesting a name for *their* group.

But all I could say was, "Um, yeah. I guess."

With a beaming smile, Hallelujah leaned into the group and said, "Then here's what we need to do."

Chapter Twenty-Five

TUESDAY, DECEMBER 6

I STUFFED MY HANDS INTO THE POCKETS OF MY WORN brown coat and kicked leaves out of my way. As I trudged toward the house, I didn't turn and wave goodbye to Uncle Ollie like I normally did when he tooted his horn at Fred Lee and me. I was too distraught to care.

I had gotten myself in a fix, as Ma Pearl would say. Why had I foolishly promised Hallelujah that I would go into town with them on Saturday and hold signs in front of Danny Ray Martin's store?

Since Reverend Jenkins would be out of town, Hallelujah thought it would be a good opportunity for us to test out a peaceful march without fear of his daddy persuading us not to.

But my knees knocked at the thought.

Dorothy and Barbara agreed to make signs out of cardboard that they had around the house, and Edward said he would nail the signs to boards. We all agreed to meet at Miss Bertha's store at eleven thirty on Saturday, then walk over to Danny Ray Martin's in time for his noontime crowd of whites who would come to enjoy the food prepared by his colored laborers, whom Hallelujah was convinced he underpaid.

I lagged behind as Fred Lee entered the house. I wasn't ready to go in. I was never ready to go in. I stopped at the porch steps and just stood there, staring at our ugly gray house.

There was a chilly wind that day. It ripped right through my coat. But the air around me was not nearly as cold as the fear in my heart. What would happen if I went into town with Hallelujah and the others and marched with signs in front of Danny Ray Martin's store? Danny Ray Martin might not have been a wealthy landowner or prominent person in Stillwater, but he was white, nonetheless. Just like Roy Bryant.

Colored folks called Roy Bryant a peckerwood, but that didn't stop a jury from claiming he was not guilty of murdering Emmett Till. Like Reverend Jenkins always said, white folks will protect their own, even if they consider them the lowest of their low.

I gazed beyond our tin-roofed shack toward the cotton fields. If Mr. Robinson found out I was causing trouble in town, he would throw us off this place. Then what? Where would we go, especially now that we had a house full of people?

Mr. Robinson had already warned Ma Pearl and Papa that if they got involved with any kind of progressive movement such as the NAACP, they might as well start looking for another place to live. I shivered, not just from the chill but from that thought. Aunt Ruthie and Slow John had been kicked off Mr. Robinson's land years ago. And they ended up living in a house that was so raggedy that it was beyond repair. And there I was, possibly about to put my grandparents in the same predicament.

I would have to back out. Just not sit with Hallelujah and his new friends. Not talk to any of them for the rest of the week. Not cause trouble for my family.

But I knew I couldn't do that, because Hallelujah wasn't going to let me.

The screen door swinging open broke my thoughts and brought me back to the moment. But Aunt Ruthie rushing out to the porch the way she did sent shivers up my arms.

"Aunt Ruthie, what's wrong?"

Breathless, holding her hand over her heart, she hurried across the porch and met me at the bottom of the steps. She reached into her dress pocket and drew out an envelope. In a whisper, she said, "I wanted to get this to you 'fo you got in the house. I didn't want Mama to see it." She sighed and gave me a contented smile. "It's a letter from Baby Susta."

My heart leaped. *"Aunt Belle?* I got a letter from Aunt Belle?"

Aunt Ruthie nodded.

My hand shook when she gave me the letter.

I stood there staring at the envelope, admiring Aunt Belle's swirling, fancy penmanship. Her address included a house number and a street name, while mine was only a route number.

I stared at the envelope for so long, Aunt Ruthie finally piped in with, "Well, ain't you go'n read it?"

I glanced up at her. "Right now?"

Aunt Ruthie motioned toward the raggedy chairs on the porch. "Sho'. Let's set right here for a spell. You can read yo' letter, and I can git me a lil' fresh air." She shrugged and added, "You don't hafta read it out loud if you don't want."

I followed her up the steps and joined her on the porch.

Not wanting to spoil its crispness, I carefully slid my finger under the seal of the envelope and opened it. "You sure you don't mind if I read it to myself?" I asked Aunt Ruthie.

She shook her head. "Nah, I'on mind."

With a smile, I read my letter.

Dear Rose,

How are you? Fine I hope. We are doing fine here. Monty and Aunt Isabelle both said to tell you hi. Monty also said to tell you "again" that he sure is sorry you won't be joining us in Saint Louis. He was looking forward to introducing you to his cousin Rhoda. She is in the 8th grade like you. You two would have gone to the same school. It's a colored school, but next year you could have gone to Beaumont High, the white school. It integrated last September, right after Topeka, Kansas. (It's not too late to change your mind, you know.)

Rhoda has been asking us a million questions about you, Rose. But she said she couldn't wait for you to get here so she could hear about life on a cotton plantation straight from the horse's mouth. She wasn't calling you a horse, of course! (Smile)

How is the weather down there? I know it's a lot warmer than it is up here. We got a lot of snow already. That's the only thing I hate about living up here. It snows almost every week in the wintertime! If you decide to come this way, make sure you have a warm coat. (Smile)

But it's worse in Chicago. Anna Mae wrote me a little while ago. She said they got snow in November. Her and Pete and Sugar and Little Man are doing real good now. She said Pete might be able to buy them a house by next summer.

Remember how I said in my last letter that I was proud of you because you are brave enough to stay in Mississippi and face the challenges of growing up among so much hate? Well, I just want to encourage you to be even stronger because things are about to get a lot worse than they already are. We heard about that poor old man Gus Courts getting shot at his store. But I am so glad that he is alive. He is one of the lucky ones! You be careful, Rose. And stay out of harm's way.

I love you! And remember, the door is still open. Anytime you are ready, you can walk right through it.

Love always,
Belle

p.s. Did y'all hear from Anna Mae yet? She said she was going to write you soon.

With a sad heart, I folded the letter and placed it back in the envelope. But what I really wanted to do was rip Aunt Belle's letter into a million pieces and let the wind blow it back to Saint Louis. She didn't even call me Rosa. I thought that she of all people would remember to call me by my new name. It made me wonder whether Monty, too, had forgotten. All that talk about nine-year-old Belle thinking of the name Rosa on the day I was born, and now only a few months after having a whole conversation about what the name meant, she had forgotten to use it.

And figure of speech or not, I still felt like Monty's cousin had called me a horse. She was probably as snobby as Ophelia, who had come down to Mississippi with them in the summer. As painful as it was to be in Mississippi, I was glad I wasn't in Saint Louis. I didn't want to have anything to do with Aunt Belle and her sophisticated Saint Louis friends.

"What she say?" Aunt Ruthie asked.

Don't be nosy, Aunt Ruthie, my heart said. But my mouth said, "She told me to be careful."

"Careful?" Aunt Ruthie asked, her brows raised.

I shrugged. "You know, so much is happening."

"Um-hmm," Aunt Ruthie said with a frown. "That po' man in Glendora wadn't doing nothin' to nobody. That man didn't hafta shoot him like that. Baby Susta sho' right. We need to be careful."

All I could think of was Aunt Belle's visit over the summer. She and Monty had spent most of their time driving around the Delta trying to convince colored people to register to vote—the same thing Mr. Gus Courts and Reverend George Lee had been shot for. How could she tell me to be careful? Why did she even care?

"Did a letter come from Mama?" I asked Aunt Ruthie.

Hesitantly, she nodded.

I sighed.

And so did Aunt Ruthie. "That's why I brung this one out to you," she said. "'Fo Mama saw it. I been tryin' my best to beat her to the mailbox every day since Anna Mae's letter came."

"Mama's letter had money in it, didn't it?"

Aunt Ruthie nodded.

"Ma Pearl still got it?"

With a pained expression, Aunt Ruthie said, "I never did see it. I heard Queen readin' it to her. Then she told her to burn it up after she read it."

"What did she say? She ask about me and Fred Lee?"

"She did," Aunt Ruthie said, nodding. "She ast how everybody was doin' and said she was sorry she couldn't send mo' money. However much it was, it still wadn't enough for Mama. She got to complainin' 'bout all the mouths she got to feed 'round here."

"Hmm," I said, sighing. "Guess she could've had one less mouth to feed if I had left in November."

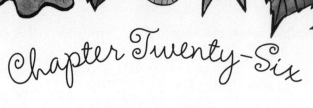

Chapter Twenty-Six

FRIDAY, DECEMBER 9

No one had seen Shorty since Monday, when he stormed out of Miss Hill's class, which is why I was so surprised to see him in the lunchroom, sitting at my usual spot, waiting for me. I had promised Hallelujah that morning that I would join them when they came in. They wanted to confirm plans for what we were now calling the March Against Discrimination at Danny Ray Martin's store. But I was too curious about Shorty and his whereabouts over the last few days to ignore him.

"Where've you been?" I asked, my tone scolding.

Shorty raised his brows. "You worried 'bout me, Lil' Cuz?"

"Of course, I am," I said. "I mean you just tore outta Miss Hill's class, and nobody's seen you since."

Shorty waved his hand. "You know I'm done with school."

"That ain't what I'm talking about."

With a sullen sigh, Shorty said, "Don't worry. I ain't shot at no white folks' houses. Yet." He gestured around the lunchroom. "Couldn't git none o' these cowards to join me nohow."

"You still working in Glendora?"

Shorty shrugged. "Nah. Mama Vee wanted me to come down from there afta the shootin'."

I pulled out my biscuits, and after offering one to Shorty (who refused), I took a bite.

"She thinks it's safer here?" I asked him.

Shorty scowled. "Lil' Cuz, it ain't safe nowhere," he said. "My granmama jest feel better 'bout me being here with them then up there where she cain't see me. Make her feel like she can keep somethin' bad from happening if I'm around."

"So what are you gonna do now?"

"Johnny Lee said he'a try to help me find somethin' here."

"Speaking of Johnny Lee," I said, "did you tell him what I said about Thanksgiving?"

Shorty's eyebrows shot up. "He'n come see y'all?"

I shook my head.

"Well, I tol' him what you said."

"What did he say?"

Shorty's forehead creased with concern. "Come to thank of it, he'n say nothin'."

Nothing. My daddy said *nothing* when Shorty told him I wanted him to come see us for Thanksgiving. Nothing. That's exactly what I felt like.

After a brief silence, Shorty said, "Heard you and Preacha' 'n'em got somethin' planned for tomorrow."

"Who told you?"

"It true?"

"Yeah," I said. Then my skin began to tingle at the thought.

Shorty shook his head. "I'on thank you oughta do it."

"Why not?"

Shorty scowled. "What good it go'n do, girl? You might git yo'self kil't."

"We're just marching."

Shorty clucked his tongue. "Ain't been but a week ago since I see'd Clinton Melton git gunned down for no reason. What you thank these peckerwoods'a do to a Negro trying to march with some signs? Look what happened to Levi for registering to vote. Dead. For no dirn reason."

"Nobody's getting shot at for marching."

"You better wise up, girl. This ain't the Nawth. These white folks down here'a gun y'all down and nobody—white or colored—go'n care. The whites'a be happy. And the coloreds be too scared to say somethin'."

He pointed his callused finger at me. "Don't forgit what happened to yo' cousin Mule. If they don't shoot you down on the street, they'a beat you down in the jail."

We both glanced toward the door when the ninth-graders began filing in. Shorty nodded toward them. "There go yo' friends. You go'n join 'em?"

I began stuffing my biscuits and a piece of fried salt pork

back into my lunch sack. "Yeah. We need to talk about to-morrow."

He placed his rough hand over mine, stopping me from packing up. "Remember what I told you," he said, his expression serious. "Don't git yo'self kil't."

I lost my appetite for the meager food I had brought for lunch. And rather than joining the conversation with Hallelujah and the others, I kept thinking about what Shorty had said.

Don't get yourself killed. Foolish me. I thought the worst that could happen was that my family might get kicked off Mr. Robinson's land. I hadn't considered somebody shooting at us while we marched outside a store.

Just as I was about to force myself to eat one of my biscuits in order to keep from starving the rest of the day, Gertrude addressed me. "You still coming, *Rosa*?"

Before I could answer, Hallelujah chimed in. "She's coming," he said, smiling. "She's our own little Rosa right here in Stillwater. And just like Mrs. Rosa Parks in Montgomery, she'll lead the way."

When Gertrude rolled her eyes, I wanted to stuff my biscuit in her face. "I don't know about leading the way," I said. "But I'll be there."

The words left my mouth, but they didn't feel real. *Be careful*, Aunt Belle had said. *Don't get killed*, Shorty had said.

We'll get thowed right off this place, I imagined Ma Pearl saying.

Why couldn't I just tell them the truth? Why couldn't I just tell them that I wasn't any braver than the rest of my family on Mr. Robinson's place? I was nothing like this Rosa lady from Montgomery. I was not willing to be thrown in jail like she and my cousin Mule had been. I didn't want to get beat up. I didn't want my ribs and my jaw broken. I wanted to be careful like Aunt Belle warned me. I wanted to live like Shorty ordered me. I wanted to make sure my family continued to have a place to live, even if it was only a shack.

I wanted to say all these things, but the smirk on Gertrude's face stopped me. She knew I was scared, and she took great pleasure in that.

My throat was dry, but I forced myself to speak. "Around eleven, right?" I asked Hallelujah.

He nodded. "Yep. Then we'll drive back to town and meet everyone else at Aunt Bertha's store."

"And we'll be there with the signs," Dorothy said, glancing at her cousin Barbara.

"Y'all scared?" Edward addressed the table.

"Lil' bit," Barbara admitted.

The other boy at the table, Floyd, finally spoke. "A lil' bit?" he said, glancing sideways at Barbara. "Shoot. I'm a whole lot scared."

"But you still coming, right?" Barbara asked him.

Floyd lowered his head and muttered, "I'on know."

The table grew silent for a moment, and I wondered whether I should speak up. Side with Floyd. Talk both our way out of going.

With clenched teeth, Hallelujah said, "We don't have room for cowards. Either take a stand or take a hike. If you ain't coming tomorrow, go on and leave now."

Floyd laughed nervously and raised his hands, palms forward. "Man, white folks shootin'. And I ain't ready to die." He stood, shook his head, and said, "I'm out."

I know it was only my imagination, but it seemed a chill crept across the table.

Hallelujah glanced from face to face. "Anybody else?"

Heads shook no.

"Everybody else in?" asked Hallelujah.

"I'm in," everyone said.

But I could only nod. My voice fled right along with my opportunity to bow out when Floyd did.

Chapter Twenty-Seven

SATURDAY, DECEMBER 10

My NERVES WERE SO JUMBLED THAT MORNING THAT I couldn't eat, even though Ma Pearl had prepared a full breakfast—biscuits, grits, eggs, and, surprisingly, bacon. But my stomach churned at the thought of food and of the task I was about to embark upon. So I bit my nails instead of biscuits.

Luckily, Ma Pearl was too busy fussing at Aunt Ruthie to concern herself with me.

Miss Bertha had come through after Hallelujah told her about my idea for Aunt Ruthie to bake cakes and sell them. On Wednesday she had supplied the necessary items to bake two pound cakes that she displayed *and sold* at her store on Friday. Today she needed two more, which provided a perfect excuse for her to send Hallelujah out to the house. To my surprise, Ma Pearl was willing to let me ride back to town with him, with strict orders that I could be gone for no more than an hour—going and coming back. I thought that reason alone would make for a short march outside Danny Ray Martin's store.

But I was wrong.

Shortly after eleven o'clock, Hallelujah carefully parked Miss Bertha's Ford on the street in front of her store. Dorothy and Barbara sat on the bench outside. With white paint, they stroked letters on their cardboard signs.

Barbara held one up. "How's this?" she asked Hallelujah.

My first thought when I read the words—"Coloreds cook here, but they can't eat here!"—was *Shouldn't you be making those inside the store instead of out here where every white person passing by can see them?*

But Hallelujah beamed and said they were perfect.

"I'll take the cakes inside," I told him.

"Both of them?"

"They're just pound cakes," I said. "I can manage."

After Hallelujah placed the two cakes on my arms, with as much care as I could, I rushed inside the store. I took deep breaths to calm myself down. How would I ever march in front of a store holding one of those signs if I couldn't bear the thought of a white person passing by and seeing them being made?

But when I entered the store, my knees nearly buckled. There, next to the counter where Miss Bertha would display Aunt Ruthie's cakes, stood Mrs. Jamison, one of the finest white citizens in all of Stillwater.

Fear rose from my heart and entered my throat, threatening to choke me. Why was Mrs. Jamison in Miss Bertha's store? And why today of all days? Could she not have come on a day when I had not been foolish enough to join my classmates in a demonstration?

I had told no one, not even Hallelujah, about my encounter with her at Mrs. Robinson's house. Through her smile, she had seemed so warm and friendly that day, so accepting of me as a fellow human being, and not just a good colored person. What would she think of me now if she saw me picking up a sign and marching back and forth in front of a white man's store protesting the way he conducted his business?

Though she was dressed as finely as she was on the day I saw her at Mrs. Robinson's, the smile she had worn was absent. Had we already done something to upset her? Had she seen Barbara and Dorothy making the signs and was planning to stop us before we even got started?

Miss Bertha's face, however, lit up when she saw me. She clasped her hands together and exclaimed, "Rosa, I'm so glad you're here!"

Please don't mention what we're about to do, I wanted to say. *Not here in front of Mrs. Jamison.* But all I could do was extend the cakes toward Miss Bertha and mutter, "I brought the cakes."

"Wonderful," she said, smiling. "Mrs. Jamison was just inquiring about Ruthie's delicious cakes. You're right on time. She wants to buy one."

"For real?" The words came out before I had time to think about them.

"Yes. For real," Miss Bertha replied with a slight chuckle.

My stomach flipped. I wanted to leap for joy. I wanted to believe that Mrs. Jamison was only there to buy a cake. But why? She had her own colored cook who could make her a cake anytime she wanted one.

I managed a smile and a nod of acknowledgment toward Miss Bertha, but I would not dare glance at Mrs. Jamison. Although I was no longer in the presence of Mrs. Robinson, the shame that she had placed in me for staring at Mrs. Jamison still lingered.

Miss Bertha patted the top of the counter and said, "You can put those right here, sweetie. One of them is lemon flavored, right?"

"Yes, ma'am," I said with a nod and a quick glance at Mrs. Jamison.

Mrs. Jamison's smile returned, as lovely as I remembered it. "I'll take the lemon one," she said, extending her delicate hands toward me. "I've tasted Pearl's lemon pound cake. I imagine her daughter's must be equally delicious."

My mouth dropped open, but no words came out. My brain kept telling my feet to move, but they wouldn't obey. I couldn't believe that of all the people of Stillwater, Mrs. Kay Marie Jamison was standing there in Miss Bertha's store, purchasing a cake that had been made by my aunt Ruthie.

"Rosa?" Miss Bertha said. "Are you okay?"

"Oh, yes, ma'am," I said, snapping to my senses. Though my legs threatened to wobble, I walked toward Mrs. Jamison with the cakes. "The lemon one is on top, ma'am," I said to her, my voice shaking.

"Thank you, dear," she replied as she took the cake. She leaned over it and inhaled. "Umm, smells divine."

After placing the other cake on the counter, I lingered inside the store, afraid to exit. No, embarrassed to exit. How could I go out there, pick up a sign, then march right past the Jamisons' store and on to Danny Ray Martin's and protest when a white woman had just supported my aunt's business?

Afraid to face the real reason I came, I sauntered over to the shelves that held canned foods. I stood there and stared at a can of yellow cling peaches as though I wanted to buy some, knowing Ma Pearl had several jars of them that she had preserved herself for the winter.

When Miss Bertha finished helping Mrs. Jamison purchase her cake and a few other items, she came over and gathered me in a hug. She smelled like new spring flowers.

She whispered in my ear, "I know you're scared. But that's what bravery is. Being scared, but doing the job anyway."

I shook my head. "I don't want to be brave. I don't want to go back out there. I don't want to do this job."

Miss Bertha held me at arm's length and said, "You can do this, Rosa. You can go out there, pick up a sign, walk a few stores down to Martin's, and march back and forth."

"What if Mrs. Jamison sees me?" I asked. "How can I go out there and do this after she just bought one of Aunt Ruthie's cakes?"

Miss Bertha scoffed. "Don't you realize that that woman is just as sick of the way colored people are being treated around here as we are?"

"Then why do they always serve their white customers first?"

Miss Bertha raised an eyebrow. "When's the last time you shopped at Jamison's?"

I shrugged. It was a very long time ago that I had visited the store with Papa and Uncle Ollie. I could still feel the eyes of the white folks who were in the store. They looked down their noses at us as though we were hogs, rather than humans, as though we had no right to shop at the same store as they. I remember that even though Papa had reached the counter with his items first, Mr. Jamison had made him step aside when a white man came to the counter after him. I re-counted the incident to Miss Bertha.

"Times have changed, Rosa," she said, softly. "And people have changed."

"Like the Jamisons?"

Miss Bertha nodded. "The Jamisons. And a few others."

"Then why do we need to march in front of Danny Ray Martin's store? Maybe he'll change too?"

"And maybe he won't," Miss Bertha said, shrugging. "The marching is not to get Danny Ray Martin to change. The marching is to demonstrate that we want change. That we will no longer stand idly by and be treated as if our lives don't matter."

I felt myself choking up. "Then why do we have to do this?" I asked. "You say 'we,' but it's us children who are about to go out there and march with signs. Why can't the grown folks do it?"

Miss Bertha creased her forehead. "Other than the fact that it was your idea?" she asked. Then she bit her lip and hesitated. She sighed and cast her eyes toward the ceiling. "You young people have less to lose. But you have so much more to gain."

I remembered what I had said when Aunt Belle and Monty came by the house after the Emmett Till murderers had been set free. Monty asked Papa why he wasn't registered to vote. Papa replied that he was too old and that he had a family to care for. Getting shot down at the courthouse won't put food on the table, he had told Monty.

"When I'm old enough," I had told them, "I'll register to vote." I had said that Papa was right. That it was the young folks who had to take a stand while we could—before we had people depending on us to take care of them.

"What was that you just said about bravery?" I asked Miss Bertha.

She smiled and said, "Bravery is when you're scared but you do the job anyway."

"Yea, though I walk through the valley of the shadow of death," I said quietly, "I will fear no evil."

Miss Bertha touched my cheek and said, "For God is with you. His rod and his staff will comfort you."

I took a deep breath and said, "And he'll prepare a table before me in the presence of my enemies."

With that, Miss Bertha hugged me again. "Now go on down there and let the people know that your enemy, Danny Ray Martin, won't allow our own people to prepare food for us."

By the time Miss Bertha and I finished, Dorothy and Barbara, along with the other girl, named Lucinda, had finished the signs and Hallelujah and Edward had nailed them to the wooden posts.

"Where's Gertrude?" I asked.

Dorothy folded her arms to her sides and flapped them up and down. "Bok, bok, bok. She chickened out."

"What!" I said. Then I remembered how only seconds ago I had wanted to do the same thing. I shrugged and said, "Some people have more to lose than others."

Barbara narrowed her eyes and said, "Or some people are just plain chicken."

"Ready, everyone?" Hallelujah asked.

With nods, we all echoed, "Ready."

People were already staring at us before we headed up the street. We didn't bother with the sidewalk because there was no sense in getting in trouble before we even started.

"Too bad we're doing this in December and not during a warmer month, like May," Dorothy said. "More people would be outside walking around instead of inside the stores."

Glancing around, I counted six people, besides us. Four of them were white. But it seemed that the two colored people were the ones who frowned at us harder. I was glad people were inside rather than out.

"Are we gonna chant?" Edward asked.

"We'll keep quiet," said Hallelujah. "Let our signs do the talking."

By the time we reached Danny Ray Martin's, my legs were shaking so bad that I thought I would collapse right there on the street. My heart beat so hard that it felt like a drumroll inside my chest.

But before we hoisted our signs and began our march, a red-faced Danny Ray Martin burst out of the store and yelled, "Don't y'all start no trouble over he'ah. I don't wanna hafta call the sheriff on y'all."

Hallelujah kept walking.

The rest of us followed.

"Git on home!" Danny Ray yelled. "This ain't the Nawth. We don't need that kinda nonsense here. Coloreds is treated fairly here in Stillwater, and y'all know it. Everybody is equal in my sto'ah."

Though Hallelujah had told us to keep silent, Barbara yelled out, "Coloreds cook here, but coloreds can't eat in your café!"

Then Edward chanted, "Coloreds can cook, but coloreds can't eat! Coloreds can cook, but coloreds can't eat!"

Barbara, Dorothy, and Lucinda joined in.

I didn't chant. Instead I whispered, "Yea, though I walk through the valley of the shadow of death, I will fear no evil."

Nor did Hallelujah chant. He sealed his lips, set his expression like stone, and marched back and forth before the store, allowing his sign to do the talking.

A few more people gathered around and stared at us. Some of them were colored. And some of them shook their heads and walked away.

Fear set in when a few of the whites began yelling at us.

"We don't need that NAACP nonsense here!" someone said.

To which Edward yelled back, "NYC! Negro Youth Council! NYC! Negro Youth Council!"

"Coloreds can cook, but coloreds can't eat! Coloreds can cook, but coloreds can't eat!" Dorothy shouted.

The chanting and the counterattacks continued for what felt like an eternity. But the worst of the yelling was when someone called out, "Ain't that the preacher's boy? Don't his daddy teach at the colored school?"

My palms got sweaty and I thought I would drop my sign. I prayed no one would call out, "Ain't that Paul and Pearl's grandchild? What's she doing here? I thought they were good Negroes."

I didn't know what time it was, but I was hoping we would soon stop. Hallelujah had promised it would be brief—just long enough to demonstrate that we had concerns. He had to get me home in time.

And he would have, if someone hadn't thrown that rock.

It landed square upside Hallelujah's head. And it knocked him flat on his back.

Chapter Twenty-Eight

MONDAY, DECEMBER 12

THE LASHING I GOT FROM MA PEARL THAT SATURDAY after I finally got home in the late afternoon should probably be written down in some record book. It was bad enough I was late, but when she found out why, I thought for sure my world was about to end, and I was about to meet my Maker.

But at least Hallelujah didn't meet his. Since Reverend Jenkins was out of town, Miss Bertha immediately closed her store and rushed Hallelujah to the hospital in Indianola—the same hospital where Gus Courts was taken when he was shot. Fortunately, Hallelujah only had a slight case of something called whiplash. The doctor said it usually occurred when people were in car accidents, but Hallelujah got it from suddenly whipping his head to the right to avoid the rock coming in from the left.

The doctor said he would have had something called a concussion if he hadn't jerked his head to the side to avoid the rock, however. He was given medicine and sent home to rest. And rather than being angry at him like Ma Pearl *and*

Papa were with me, Reverend Jenkins was proud that his son had suffered for what he considered a just cause.

None of us had spoken since the incident, so I was unsure whether we would meet during lunchtime that Monday. Hallelujah was still resting, but Reverend Jenkins had said Miss Bertha would bring him to school later in the day if he felt like attending. I had my fingers crossed that he would show up, but I got a surprise lunch companion instead—Shorty.

It was the first time since he'd quit coming to school that I didn't want to see him. I was sure he would only make fun of us for what seemed like a failed attempt to march, or demonstrate, as Reverend Jenkins called it.

So before he sat down, I tried to turn him away. "I'm saving that seat for Hallelujah."

Shorty shook his head. "Ninth grade don't come in here for another ten minutes. We got plenty time to talk. Plus, from what I hear, Preacha' won't be showin' up anyway."

I tried rudeness. "Why are you here? I thought you quit school."

Shorty scoffed. "I ain't here for no learnin'. I'm here to see you."

"Well, if you're here to talk about what happened on Saturday, then you can just leave. I don't wanna talk about it."

"Then I'll stay," said Shorty. "'Cause I ain't here to talk about what y'all did on Saturday. I'm here to talk to you 'bout yo' daddy."

My mood suddenly perked up. "What about him?"

"I talked to him yesterday. Ast him why he'n come see you and yo' brother on Thanksgiving. Said he got too busy and couldn't make it out there. He had to take his wife over to Kilmichael to see her family. By the time they got back, he said it was too late to be visitin' folks."

"Where's Kilmichael? Is it far?" I asked.

"It's a good ways past Greenwood. It's kinda far."

I nodded. "Okay."

"I ast him 'bout Christmas," Shorty said. "Said he'a try to make it out there then."

"What about—"

Shorty cut me off. "He said he ain't comin' out there no other time. 'Nuff white folks gunnin' down Negroes. He'on need to git gunned down by no mean-as-the-devil colored woman like yo' granmama."

I smiled at the thought of my daddy dropping by on Christmas morning. He might even bring me and Fred Lee gifts. But then I remembered how Ma Pearl had reacted to the knock at the door on Thanksgiving when she thought it might be Aunt Ruthie's husband, Slow John. She said that he better not dare show up at her house. I now wondered if the same was true of Johnny Lee.

I shook my head. "I don't know if he can come see us. Not even for Christmas."

Shorty frowned. "Look, girl. You wanna see yo' daddy or not?"

I nodded. "I do. But—"

"Then stop worrying 'bout yo' granmama," Shorty said with a wave of his hand. "Let him come."

"Okay," I said, nodding but still feeling nervous.

"I'll be sho' to remind him on Christmas Eve. Make sho' he come see y'all," Shorty said, smiling. "I thank you and him go'n git 'long real good."

"I hope so," I said.

Christmas was two weeks away, but I already felt butterflies in my stomach. What if Shorty was wrong? What if me and my daddy didn't get along *real good*? What if he didn't like me at all? What if I didn't like him?

On the other hand, what if we did get along, and he wanted to start seeing me and Fred Lee more? Would Ma Pearl let him? I bet Papa would. Maybe Johnny Lee would even take us to his house sometimes, unlike Mama, who never did. I just hope our little sisters and brother weren't spoiled rotten like Sugar and Lil' Man. And I certainly hoped

Johnny Lee wouldn't make them refer to me and Fred Lee as Aunt Rose and Uncle Fred as Mama had done with Sugar and Lil' Man.

Before I continued to let my imagination run free with thoughts of a future relationship with my daddy, Shorty surprised me. He placed his hand on my shoulder. "Tell the lil' preacha' that I'm proud o' him."

"Huh?"

Shorty nodded. "I'm proud of all y'all. What y'all did took guts. Jenkins lucky that was a rock that came at him and not a bullet. I done see'd for myself what these white peoples'a do. They'a gun a Negro down in open daylight and won't thank twice 'bout it. I'm glad Lil' Jenkins doing okay."

Shorty placed his rough hand over mine. "I'm glad all y'all okay."

All I could say was "Thank you."

"Well, Lil' Cuz," Shorty said, rising from his seat, "I won't be bothering you no mo'. I won't be comin' back up here interrupting yo' lunchtime with Jenkins. I'm movin' on. Go'n mind my own bizness. Try to leave these white folks 'lone."

"No more thoughts of going out at night shooting at windows?" I asked him.

Shorty shook his head. "Nah. You and Jenkins right. Wouldn't do nothin' but make them madder. Jest make thangs harder on the folks that got to live on they land and tend to they crops every summer. Make it harder on the folks that got to clean up they houses and raise they chi'rens for 'em.

"I could shoot at they windows at night and scare 'em all I want. But it ain't go'n change nothin'. The ones full o' hate ain't go'n never leave Negroes 'lone. They go'n keep on terrorizin' us."

I was so happy to see Hallelujah when the ninth-graders entered the lunchroom that I almost leaped out of my seat. But I didn't have to go to him; he immediately turned in my direction and headed over—not even bothering to stop in the short line to get food.

Just as I was about to ask him how he was feeling, he slumped down beside me with a huff. He shook his head and said through gritted teeth, "I can't believe what I just overhead."

"What?"

"Dr. Howard is leaving."

"Leaving what?"

Hallelujah narrowed his eyes. "Mississippi."

My stomach knotted. "Dr. Howard? From Mound Bayou?"

Hallelujah frowned. "Do you know of another Dr. Howard?"

"He's leaving Mississippi?"

Hallelujah gave me a *didn't I just say that* kind of stare.

"Why is he leaving?" I asked.

"The same reason everyone else left. He's a coward."

I grinned and said, "Then maybe that's what we should call him from now on—Dr. Coward instead of Dr. Howard."

"Do you think this is a joke?"

I was about to respond with a joke, but the look in Hallelujah's eyes made me pause. He looked as if he would cry at any moment.

I held up my hand. "Wait. Slow down. First of all, how are you feeling? Is your head better?"

"It's not my head. It's my neck," Hallelujah said tersely. "I didn't have a concussion. I had whiplash from turning my head too quickly. Stupid rock almost hit me in the eye. And yes, my neck is better. But I'm not."

I glanced around. "Where are Edward and Lucinda?"

Hallelujah shrugged. "Not here, I guess."

"Hmm. Dorothy and Barbara didn't come today either."

Hallelujah's shoulders drooped. "I feel like a failure. And a fool. Here I am bragging about Dr. Howard and how he moved the folks in Montgomery to take a stand. Now he's running away like everyone else, like our little *NYC*," he said with a dismissive wave of his hand.

"I'm here."

Hallelujah squinted at me. "Yeah. I'm surprised Miss Sweet let you out of the house."

"She gave me enough licks from that strap of hers. Guess she figured that lashing oughta last me for a while."

Hallelujah dropped his face in his palms. "I can't believe I got you into all this trouble for nothing." He moaned into his hands and said, "I was making fun of Shorty Cooper for wanting to shoot at white folks' houses, but I bet he's laughing at me now."

"No," I said, shaking my head. "He said he was proud of you."

Hallelujah glanced up. "He did?"

I nodded. "He said that what we did took a lot of guts. He even begged me not to do it. He was worried I might get killed."

Hallelujah exhaled an exasperated sigh. "I shouldn't have been so puffed up with pride," he said. "You were right. I was classing myself. I judged Shorty without bothering to get to know him."

Hallelujah really looked like he might cry now. "I did the same thing," I said quickly. "I judged him too. So stop beating yourself up about it."

"I just can't believe so much is happening right now,"

he said, shaking his head. "Folks are getting killed. And I feel like we can't do anything about it. Maybe that's why Dr. Howard is leaving. Maybe the boycott isn't enough. Maybe he doesn't think it will change anything."

"Or . . . maybe he's going to Montgomery. You know, to *help* with the bus boycott."

Hallelujah shook his head. "Nope. Either Chicago or California. The word is that he's been spending a lot of time out there already."

"California? That's where Shorty's mama is."

Ignoring my comment, Hallelujah threw up his hands. "Why are we even doing this? What's the point? We're getting hit by rocks. People are getting shot. And fighters like Dr. Howard are packing up and leaving. Maybe that's what we all should do—just pack our bags and leave."

I shook my head. "You don't mean that."

Hallelujah nodded. "I do."

"But even you said that we all can't leave. Somebody has to stay and fight for those who really can't leave."

"Then maybe we should find a way for all the Negroes to leave the South," Hallelujah said, his face set in a tight frown.

"You don't mean that either," I said. "Besides, I don't want to leave. As crazy as that sounds. I feel like I have a right to live here, just like any white person."

Hallelujah groaned.

I kept trying. "Don't you like hearing the birds singing in the trees at dawn?"

"Birds are everywhere," he answered.

"I bet whippoorwills aren't. Don't you enjoy hearing them sing in the evenings?"

Hallelujah rolled his eyes. "They're noisy."

"But isn't the evening hoot of an owl peaceful?"

"Nope."

I sighed. "Would you really want to live in the city with all those tall buildings and a bunch of concrete everywhere?"

Hallelujah answered crisply, "There're some spacious places in the North, too. Every inch isn't covered with tall buildings and concrete."

"What about the nighttime? Don't you like being able to go outside, stare up at the darkness, and see a sky full of stars?"

Hallelujah shrugged. "Stars are everywhere too. I can see them in Ohio just like I can see them in Mississippi."

I threw up my hands. "I give up, Hallelujah Jenkins. Go ahead, run up north. Desert the people who need you. Desert them like your hero Dr. Howard is doing." I gestured toward the lunchroom window. "Go ahead. Leave."

"I wish I could feel the way you do. But I don't right now."

"I can't believe I'm talking to the bravest boy I know, and you want to quit because somebody else has."

"You don't understand. I put so much faith in Dr. Howard. He was my hero."

"Your daddy is always preaching about not putting our faith in man, not even him."

With a sigh, Hallelujah said, "Because man will let you down."

"So put your trust in?"

"God," said Hallelujah. "And God alone."

"Man can help us, but?"

With a slight smile and a tiny sigh, Hallelujah said, "Man can't save us."

I nodded. "Now you better get some food. Lunch'll be over before you know it."

He nodded toward my lunch sack. "I think we should both try to eat. No point in starving just because Dr. Coward is running away from the fight."

I grabbed my biscuit from my lunch sack. "I'm glad you're feeling better," I said.

"And I'm glad we're all safe. At least it was only a rock that came at me and not a bullet." Hallelujah paused, then winced. "And at least it hit me and not one of you. Edward was right behind me. It could've hit him."

"It was terrible, regardless," I said.

"But Edward's mama and daddy might not have been able to take him to the hospital if he had gotten hurt," Hallelujah said. He stared down at the table and was quiet for a moment. When he finally looked up, he had tears in his eyes. "It was bad enough I got everyone in trouble. I could never forgive myself if someone had gotten hurt."

Chapter Twenty-Nine

THURSDAY, DECEMBER 15

Because I was always so tired by day's end, I rarely had trouble falling asleep. But this night I tossed and turned, unable to block the turmoil of life's events from my head.

Dorothy and Barbara returned to school that day, but they had avoided me. At lunchtime they returned to their usual spot. The others did the same. It looked like NYC had become the new MIA. We were officially missing in action.

And according to Hallelujah, so was Dr. Howard. Several newspapers reported that he had, indeed, left Mississippi. Sold eight hundred acres of his land. His house too. And was gone, just like that. To California.

"They will take me out in a wooden box," he had said. Yet, he was leaving because he didn't want to get killed.

If someone as important to the movement as Dr. Howard could leave, then who was I to stay? We were such chickens in Stillwater that one rock had caused us to run.

I was glad I hadn't ripped Aunt Belle's letter to pieces. I had pulled it from beneath my mattress—my hiding spot

—several times over the last few days to read it. Well, one sentence of it anyway: *Remember, the door is still open. Anytime you are ready, you can walk right through it.*

I wanted other people to fight. I wanted Dr. Howard to risk his life. I wanted people like Rosa Parks—even that preacher, Martin Luther King—to take risks for me. I wanted people like Reverend Jenkins and my seventh grade teacher, Miss Johnson, to boldly speak of change and progression for the Negro in their classrooms. I wanted Miss Bertha to run a store and be hated by white folks for doing so. But there I was, thinking about leaving again.

When I flipped over for what was probably the twentieth time in one hour, Queen stirred and sat up in her bed. "You still woke?" she asked.

"Mm-hmm," I said, rolling onto my back.

"You been to sleep at all?"

I propped my pillow against the wall and sat up in bed. "Nope. Been woke since I got in the bed."

"Me too," Queen said.

Her voice sounded unusually sad.

"The baby keeping you awake?" I asked.

"This baby and everything else. I ain't slept in days."

"You in pain?"

"Not my body," Queen answered. "But my heart feel like somebody done tore it to pieces."

"You still thinking about Jimmy Robinson?"

A choked sob cut through the darkness.

"Queen?"

Only broken sobs answered me.

I eased off my bed, careful not to make too much noise with my squeaking mattress and springs. I slid beside Queen and placed my arm around her shaking shoulders.

"Shh," I said. "You don't wanna wake Ma Pearl."

"I don't care," Queen said. "She ain't go'n do nothin' but fuss anyway. That's all she do all day. Fuss at me and Aunt Ruthie and these chi'ren. You lucky you get to go to school and don't have to hear her grumblin' and complainin' all day."

"That why you crying?"

"A lil' bit," Queen said, her crying calming down to sniffles.

"What's the rest? You crying because Jimmy don't come see you anymore?"

"I ain't stud'n him!" Queen hissed.

"Then what is it?"

"I don't want my baby —"

Fresh sobs broke her words. She snatched up her sheets and cried into them.

"Me and Aunt Ruthie will help you take care of the baby," I said.

Queen shook her head from side to side. "Nah. That

wadn't what I was saying." She sniffed. "I don't want my baby growin' up in this house. I wanna leave."

"Maybe Aunt Belle could come get you."

"She don't want nobody but you," Queen said with a hint of anger in her tone. "She ain't go'n take no knocked-up girl like me to the city and shame her. She want somebody smart like you. Somebody she can show off to her city friends. Somebody to brag about."

I pulled back from her. "Me? Why would she brag about me?"

"You smart and you got sense 'nuff to stay outta trouble."

Even though she was complimenting me, there was still a bit of anger in her voice.

"And you did that thing Saturday," she said. "You went to town with Hallelujah and marched with them signs. That's something Baby Susta would do. She would be proud of you. Ain't nobody proud of me."

I didn't know how to answer Queen. I was happy that she felt that way about me but sad that she felt that way about herself.

"Maybe you should write Aunt Belle," I said. "Ask her if you could come to Saint Louis. You won't know how she feels about you unless you ask. She might be proud of me, but it seemed like she liked you more. She brought you prettier clothes."

"Them just clothes. They don't mean nothin'. You the one she brags about."

I couldn't believe the next words that came out of my mouth. "She wrote me and said I could still go to Saint Louis if I wanted to. But I don't want to. Maybe she'll let you come in my place. Maybe after you have the baby. Maybe you could leave the baby with Aunt Clara Jean."

"I wouldn't leave my baby here. My baby goin' wherever I go. I wouldn't ever do my baby like my mama did me."

I immediately felt bad for even suggesting such a thing. I knew that pain of being left behind. Just like Queen. Just like Fred Lee. Just like Shorty.

"I'm sorry," I said. "I wasn't thinking."

"I know," Queen answered. "You was just thinking about what might be the best for me. A way for me to start a new life."

"I guess so," I said, shrugging.

Queen rubbed her stomach. "This baby is part of my new life, wherever that might be." She sighed and scooted back down under her covers. "I need to try to get some sleep. You too. You still got school to go to."

I trudged back to my own bed and sank under my covers. I was wide awake, not sure whether sleep would come to me at all. Despite the differences Queen and I had had in the past, I truly felt sorry for her. Sorry for her yet proud of her at the same time. Even if she cared for no one else, she cared for her child who would soon be born. She cared enough that she wouldn't leave him—or her—behind and start a new life without him.

When I flipped to my side, trying to get comfortable, Queen stirred again. "Rose?" she called.

I sat up. "Yes?"

"Would you write her for me?"

"Aunt Belle?"

"Yeah," Queen said, her voice sounding really sad. "Would you write her and ask her if she would take me and my baby in?"

Without a second thought, I answered, "Yes."

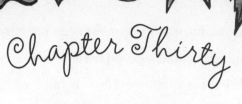

Chapter Thirty

TUESDAY, DECEMBER 20

Despite my often bleak circumstances, the week of Christmas was normally a happy time for me. The house was always filled with the scent of baking cakes and the sounds of Christmas carols coming through the static of Ma Pearl's radio. But the Christmas of 1955 was different. For one, Aunt Ruthie was there, and her cake business was thriving. Of course, that created a problem for Ma Pearl because the kitchen was where she spent most of her time during that week.

Aunt Ruthie had seven cakes to bake before Christmas Eve, and Ma Pearl was not allowing her to use her kitchen. It was early morning, only minutes after Slick Charlie had awakened us with a crow. School was out for the winter break, so I sat on the porch with Aunt Ruthie—despite the chill—and pondered how she would get cakes baked without a kitchen.

Quilts warmed the outside of our bodies while hot coffee warmed the inside. The sounds of slinging pots and pans traveled from the kitchen to the front porch, reminding us that Ma Pearl was now in command—her cakes would get baked, while Aunt Ruthie's would not.

I took a careful sip of coffee but still burned my lip. "I bet Mrs. Robinson would have let Ma Pearl use her kitchen if she'd asked."

Aunt Ruthie grunted. "That white woman don't love her that much. She ain't lettin' her cook her own food over there." She shook her head. "She can cook all the cakes she want for them, but I ain't never heard of a white woman lettin' a colored woman use her kitchen to cook for her own family."

"Can you make the cakes at Miss Bertha's house?"

Aunt Ruthie, sipping her coffee, shook her head. "How I'm s'posed to git to Bertha's? I cain't even git my own chi'ren to town to go to school."

"Have you asked her?"

"Course I ain't."

"Maybe she'll take you."

Aunt Ruthie shrugged. "Too late now. How I'm s'posed to git in touch with her? We ain't got no telephone. When she dropped off the supplies and the orders, I didn't know Mama wadn't go'n let me use the kitchen. Now I'm jest stuck." She shook her head. "I got all these orders. All these peoples want me to make cakes for them for Christmas, and I don't have no kitchen to work in."

The Robinsons had a telephone. Papa had asked to use it

occasionally when he needed to get in touch with Reverend Jenkins. Other than that, none of us had ever asked to use their telephone.

Aunt Ruthie glared at me from the corner of her eye. "No," she said sternly. "I ain't astin' Miz Robinson to use her telephone." She took a sip of coffee. "Besides, Papa says don't ast the white folks for nothin' 'less it's a emergency."

"This is an emergency, Aunt Ruthie! You've got seven cakes to bake and no way to bake them. You need to call Miss Bertha so she can pick you up and take you to her house."

Aunt Ruthie only shook her head.

"Then how about Uncle Ollie," I suggested. "Maybe he could give you a ride to town."

"Girl, what I'm s'posed to do? Show up at Bertha's sto' and ast to go to her house and use her kitchen?"

After we both giggled for a moment, Aunt Ruthie sighed and stared in the direction of the Robinsons' house. "I guess I could walk on over there at a decent time after the sun all the way up and ast to use the telephone." She shrugged. "Cain't hurt nothin'. All Miz Robinson can do is say, 'Yes, c'mon in,' or 'No, and don't never come over here both'rin' me again.'"

We both laughed again before taking sips of coffee.

Aunt Ruthie nodded. "I'll jest call Bertha and let her

know thangs ain't goin' too good here and see if I can come to her house. Thank I'll jest git Ollie to take me 'stead of Bertha havin' to come out here and git me."

"Good for you, Aunt Ruthie," I said. "And you know me and Queen and Fred Lee will watch the children while you're gone."

And with that, she smiled at me and said, "Now what 'bout you?"

"What about me?" I asked.

"Oh, Rose," she said, holding her hand over her heart and shaking her head, "why you stay, baby? How come you didn't let Belle come back for you?"

Aunt Ruthie's words hit me like a surprise summer storm. I didn't know what to say, so I simply shrugged and said, "I didn't want to go to Saint Louis. I wanted to stay here. With my family."

"Belle family," Aunt Ruthie answered. "Aunt Isabelle too. And might as well say that ol' talk-too-much Monty is family since they 'bout to be married soon."

When I didn't say anything, Aunt Ruthie said, "Rose, you could have a good life."

"I—" I stopped. I couldn't even force the lie out of my mouth. I didn't have a good life. I had a miserable life. I had no mama. I had no daddy. I had a grandma who one minute

acted as if she despised my very skin, then in the next minute acted as if she didn't want to see any harm come to me
because I *was* her own flesh and blood. Then there was Papa.
He cared. He loved me more than anyone else did. Yet . . . I
couldn't bring myself to think the thought.

"You so smart," Aunt Ruthie continued. "You could go to
a good school."

"I go to a good school," I said. "We might have old stuff,
but we have good teachers. Reverend Jenkins and Miss
Johnson are very good teachers."

Aunt Ruthie nodded. "That may be so. But what 'bout
some o' the others?"

My forehead creased. "They all went to college."

"That ain't what I'm talkin' 'bout," Aunt Ruthie said. "Is
they teachin' the history?"

"The history?"

"Not the one where we was slaves. The real one. The one
white folks don't want y'all to know."

"Aunt Ruthie—"

She cut me off. "You didn't thank I cared, did you?"

I shook my head. "No, ma'am. I didn't."

"Oh, Rose. I care. I care deeply. You know how bad I
wanted to go to Saint Louis when I was sixteen?"

I shook my head.

"I snuck in the trunk o' the car," Aunt Ruthie said, smiling at the memory. "Aunt Isabelle 'n'em didn't know I was in there till they stopped in Memphis."

"Why'd they stop?"

Aunt Ruthie chuckled and said, "I couldn't breathe and started banging on the trunk to git out."

"Aunt Ruthie! You could've died!"

"Well, I didn't. And they brought me right on back here to this house." She shook her head. "I wanted to go so bad."

"I did too," I said quietly. "At first."

"How come you changed yo' mind?"

I shrugged. "Lots of reasons. Papa. Fred Lee. This," I said, gesturing toward the open space.

"Rose, you kiddin' me, ain't you?"

Sheepishly, I shook my head.

"You stayed for this?" Aunt Ruthie said, frowning. When I didn't answer, she shook her head. "Rose, baby, land is everywhere. You need to think about yo' future. What kind of future do you have here?"

I stared squint-eyed at her. "You ever been to Mound Bayou?"

"No. But I heard of it."

"You know it was founded by Negroes?"

"That's what I hear peoples say."

I told Aunt Ruthie about Joe Ann.

"College? At sixteen?"

I nodded. "I wanna do that too."

"I bet you could do it faster if you was in Saint Louis."

"Joe Ann said there were other students from the Delta at her college. Some are sharecroppers' children."

Aunt Ruthie nodded. "That's real nice, Rose. But I still wants to know why you is so scared to go to Saint Louis."

"I ain't—"

"You scared, chile."

I shook my head. "No, Aunt Ruthie. I'm not. At first I was."

I told her about the conversation I had overhead at Mrs. Robinson's, and how bad it had made me feel. "They made me feel as dumb as a rock, like I really was worthless because I'm a Negro. Then I went to Mound Bayou and saw what was possible. I saw a great work that had been done by former slaves, and I knew my people weren't as dumb as rocks, because rocks don't build cities.

"And I want to be like Joe Ann. I want to go to a fine colored college like Tougaloo. I know it's too late for me to go at sixteen, but I want to be one of those Delta sharecropper children at Tougaloo."

"I still don't understand you," Aunt Ruthie said, smiling.

"But I'll accept what you say, 'cause you sho' don't sound scared to me."

I shook my head. "I'm not, Aunt Ruthie. I was before, but I'm not anymore." I thought about how disappointed Hallelujah was to find out Dr. Howard was leaving Mississippi. I thought about how heartbroken I was when Mama left me and Fred Lee. "I want to be here for my family," I said. "I want to help you get your business started. I want you to be like Miss Bertha and the colored folks in Mound Bayou who have their own stores. I want to help you with your children."

Aunt Ruthie placed her mug on the floor of the porch. I did the same, as the coffee was no longer hot. She smiled at me warmly. "Rose, that's beautiful," she said. "You have a heart of gold. But you don't hafta stay here for me and my chi'ren. We'll be a'right. You need to do what's right for you. You jest thirteen, baby. You got yo' whole life ahead o' you. You can be more than any o' us ever wanted to be."

"And I will be," I said. "And I can do it right here. In Mississippi. With my family. Besides, with any luck, Queen might get to go to Saint Louis." I told Aunt Ruthie about the letter I had written to Aunt Belle on Queen's behalf and how I had gotten Hallelujah to mail it for me so Ma Pearl wouldn't find out.

Aunt Ruthie smiled. "You full o' surprises, Rose. Jest like

yo' mama. Anna Mae might not had the book smarts like you, but she sho' know how to make a way outta no way."

"Well, hopefully Aunt Belle will let Queen go live in Saint Louis."

Aunt Ruthie glanced toward the door. "I hope so too," she said.

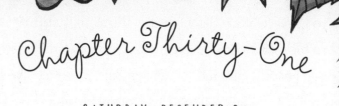

Chapter Thirty-One

SATURDAY, DECEMBER 24

A BABY DOLL. IT WAS ALL I EVER WANTED FOR Christmas. But I never got one.

Once, while playing in the yard when I was six years old, I found a small tree branch that had twigs sticking out to the sides like arms. I took the branch inside with me and pretended its top was a head, the twigs were arms, and the bottom was legs, one draped over the other. I wrapped the branch in a little blue and white quilt I found in the trunk in Grandma Mandy's room.

It was almost as if my six-year-old self knew I would never actually own a doll, so I played with the tree branch as though she were one. I held her in my lap. I sang to her. I tried to read the funny pages to her. I even slept with her —until Mama made me throw her away.

A year later she left me and Fred Lee for Sugar and Lil' Man. She should have let me keep my tree-doll. At least I would have had something to hug when she was no longer there.

Now, seven years later, at age thirteen, I still secretly wished for a doll when Reverend Jenkins came on Christmas morning bearing gifts for me, Queen, and Fred Lee. He had been bringing us gifts since I was nine—young enough to still want a doll. So I'm not sure why a doll never made its way into the box he presented us. Perhaps it was because my best friend was a boy, and he assumed I didn't like dolls. Or perhaps he remembered how much I used to love climbing the ancient oak in the front yard way more than Hallelujah did. Then again, there was that one time I cried because Fred Lee received a slingshot and I received a book. As much as I wanted the slingshot, the real reason for my tears was because I didn't want the book. I was so mad that I don't even remember what the book was about, or what happened to it.

But this year Reverend Jenkins came by on Christmas Eve rather than Christmas Day. It was one in the afternoon when they showed up. I had spent the day sweeping and mopping every floor in the house except the kitchen. And that's because both Ma Pearl and Aunt Ruthie bustled about in there preparing a feast as if Jesus himself would show up at our front door on Christmas Day.

The house was warm and cozy and filled with a mixture of sweet smells and salty and spicy ones. My mouth watered at the thought of Ma Pearl's chicken dressing with a slice of coconut cake on the side. Christmas was the only day that we were allowed to eat dessert anytime we wanted even if it meant having it on the same plate as our regular meal. And I had promised myself that I would not let ingratitude spoil Christmas like I had Thanksgiving, even if Mr. Robinson sent over another consolation turkey. So far that week we hadn't seen one.

I had just left my room, where I had changed into a clean dress, when I heard the voices of Hallelujah, Reverend Jenkins, and Miss Bertha in the parlor. My heart rejoiced. Miss Bertha was visiting us too!

She had allowed Aunt Ruthie the use of her kitchen for two days so she could fulfill her Christmas cake orders. In addition to the first order of seven cakes she had received on Monday, seven more orders came in the next day. And like a champ, Aunt Ruthie had gotten those seven cakes baked and ready for pickup at the store on the day before Christmas Eve.

To keep Aunt Ruthie from being tempted to use any of the money she earned from her cakes, Miss Bertha and Reverend Jenkins agreed to pool their money and buy small toys for each of her children. (I secretly hoped the girls would get dolls, so I could play with them too.) The Jenkinses truly were good people, and not just good *colored* people. Well, in the opinion of most whites, they probably weren't good colored people anyway, seeing how they wouldn't "stay in their place."

The voices coming from the parlor weren't as festive as I expected. Papa, Ma Pearl, and Aunt Ruthie had congregated in there as well. When I approached the doorway, they all stopped talking and stared at me awkwardly. Had I done something wrong?

One look at Aunt Ruthie told me the answer to that question was no.

She was sitting on the sofa, sobbing.

Miss Bertha sat next to her, her arm draped around Aunt Ruthie's shoulders. She looked as if she had been sobbing too.

My first thought was that something bad had happened to Slow John. And I felt guilty. For years I had hoped something bad would happen to that man—even death—just to get him out of my aunt's life. But what if he had been lynched? No matter how evil Slow John was, the thought of even him being killed just because of the color of his skin made me nauseous.

I wrapped my arms around my stomach and pressed away the sickness.

The chair creaked when Ma Pearl hoisted herself out of it. She stood, shoulders slumped, and sighed. She shook her head and said, "I'm a go'n back in here 'n finish cookin'.

"I'm so sick o' this mess," she said as she brushed past me, almost knocking me over.

I entered the parlor and sat in the chair that had been warmed by Ma Pearl. "What happened?" I asked.

Miss Bertha stared at me with solemn eyes. "Someone set fire to my store last night."

I gasped.

"Oh, Rose!" Aunt Ruthie wailed. "All my cakes is gone!"

"Someone burned up your cakes?" I asked.

"No," Hallelujah answered for Aunt Ruthie. "Vandals tried to burn down Aunt Bertha's store."

"What?" I grabbed my chest because an almost unbearable pain had invaded it. "How?"

"Someone poured gasoline at the back door and lit it," Reverend Jenkins said. "Luckily Mr. Jamison was still at his store doing inventory and noticed a brightness that shouldn't have been there. When he saw the fire, he didn't bother calling the police. He already knew they'd do nothing.

"He called me. And I called Bertha. When we got to the store, Jamison had already rounded up a bunch of folks, both colored and white, and they were putting out the fire with buckets of water." He shook his head and said, "I thank God for that man. He's one of the few whites around here who hasn't joined that Citizens' Council."

"A lot of stuff was still destroyed though," said Miss Bertha, choking up. "Including all those cakes Ruthie worked so hard on."

"Cakes can be replaced," said Papa. "Let's jest thank the good Lawd that it wasn't peoples they destroyed this time."

"Amen," said Hallelujah.

"I knowed this was all too good to be true," Ma Pearl said as she reentered the parlor. Again she had managed to slip into the room without being noticed.

Without her telling me to, I knew to get out of the chair she had been sitting in. I joined Aunt Ruthie and Miss Bertha on the sofa.

"How you know this ain't the Lawd's way o' tellin' you you ain't got no bizness makin' cakes up in somebody's kitchen then turnin' right 'round tryin' to sell 'em to peoples. Somethin' jest ain't right 'bout that."

"It's called entrepreneurship, Miss Sweet," said Reverend Jenkins. "And people have been doing it since Bible times. When the widow of a prophet had to pay off her husband's debts, the prophet Elisha asked her what she had in her home. She replied that all she had was one jar of oil. The prophet told her to go borrow jars from all her neighbors, then pour the oil from her jar into the other jars. By a miracle, the oil from that one jar filled all the others. Then the prophet told her to go sell those jars of oil to her neighbors so that she could pay off her deceased husband's debts and then she and her sons could live off the rest.

"And that is just what Ruthie has done. She has taken what she has — her baking skills — and she is using that to earn a living for herself and her children after her no-count husband — who is as good as dead to her — has left them with nothing to live off." Reverend Jenkins stared lovingly at Aunt Ruthie and said, "And you should be proud of her."

Ma Pearl grunted and said, "Did the Bible say anything 'bout that widow's oil burning up? If this was from the Lawd, then how come them cakes burnt up 'fo peoples had a chance to come git 'em?"

"Because we live in a world where evil abounds, Miss Sweet," said Reverend Jenkins. "And sometimes the good gets mixed right in with it. But trust me, the cream always rises back to the top no matter how much you stir it up with the clabber."

"Well, Mr. Fancy Words, today Christmas Eve, so how she go'n git seven cakes fixed and took to the folks that done already paid for 'em?"

Papa cleared his throat. "Last I checked," he said, "there was exactly seven cakes sittin' there in the safe in the kitchen. They already covered up with plastic and ready to go."

"Them my cakes!" Ma Pearl snapped.

"You don't need 'em," answered Papa. "Look like you could stand to miss a few meals anyway."

"Y'all ain't takin' nan' one o' my cakes outta my kitchen," said Ma Pearl.

Papa addressed Miss Bertha. "When you need to git them cakes delivered to Ruthie's customers?"

Miss Bertha glanced at Ma Pearl, who huffed as she crossed her arms over her chest. "I think the customers will understand. We can't help if someone set fire to the store."

"Rose," Papa said to me, "you 'n this boy go on in there and git them cakes and put 'em in Preacher's car."

Hallelujah looked as if he was scared to move. But I wasn't. I jumped up off the sofa and strutted straight across the floor.

With much hesitation, Hallelujah followed.

After three trips, we had loaded six of the cakes into Reverend Jenkins's car. The last cake left in the safe was the big white coconut one. It had three sumptuous layers of moist yellow cake with plenty of vanilla cream between each layer and an abundance of coconut packed into the outer layer. I didn't want it to go.

When Hallelujah reached into the safe and pulled it out, my mouth watered.

"I wonder who's getting that one," I said.

Hallelujah shrugged. "I don't know. But folks have been going crazy over Miss Ruthie's cakes, so I hope Miss Sweet's cakes are just as good."

I wiped drool from the corner of my mouth. "That one is," I said, sighing.

Ma Pearl stormed into the kitchen, grumbling. "Now what I'm s'posed to do 'bout cakes tomorra'?"

Maybe Mr. Robinson can buy us one. "If you have the ingredients, I'll help you make another coconut cake," I offered.

"Humph" was all Ma Pearl said before she turned and stalked back out of the kitchen.

"What'll Miss Bertha do now?" I asked Hallelujah as we headed to the car with that delicious coconut cake.

"Pick up the pieces and move on like she always does," he answered. "And don't worry. She'll make sure Miss Ruthie is able to keep making cakes and selling them. She doesn't need a store for that. Just a kitchen."

"I just hope Aunt Ruthie doesn't give up," I said.

"Don't worry. Aunt Bertha won't let her."

"You think people will still buy Aunt Ruthie's cakes after Christmas?"

Hallelujah frowned. "Course they will. Aunt Bertha says even a few white folks have asked about Miss Ruthie's cakes." He carefully placed the cake on the back seat with the others. "Besides, Aunt Bertha has even bigger plans for Miss Ruthie. But she's waiting until after New Year to tell her." He raised one eyebrow. "Can you keep a secret?"

"I've been known to accomplish it once or twice," I answered.

Even though there was no one else besides me who would hear him, Hallelujah leaned in and whispered, "Aunt Bertha's making arrangements for Miss Ruthie to move to town so she won't have to pay Miss Sweet to use her kitchen."

My heart leaped. "Wait. If Aunt Ruthie moves to town, Lil' John and Virgil can go to school."

Hallelujah nodded. "Yep. They sure can." He grinned and said, "And it's all because of you."

"Me?"

"You suggested to your aunt that she bake cakes and sell 'em. Now look where it's leading to — her maybe having her own business and her children finally going to school."

I had heard people say that their hearts swelled with pride.

Well, for the first time in my thirteen—almost fourteen—
years, I experienced it for myself. Hallelujah was right. I had
encouraged Aunt Ruthie to use her skills to help herself. And
I felt good, like a bright shining star on a moonless night.

Chapter Thirty-Two

SUNDAY, DECEMBER 25

I was glad Christmas came on a Sunday that year. Church service wasn't as long as it was on a regular Sunday because Reverend Jenkins wanted to make sure we had sufficient time to spend with our families that day. And he wanted to make sure the few children who received toys from "Santa Claus" actually had time to enjoy them. And for the "bad" ones who received only coal in their stockings, he had said, he hoped they could find a use for that too.

Aunt Belle used to do that to me and Fred Lee when we were little—put coal in our socks. She stopped when I asked her why Santa didn't like us. At first, I thought Santa didn't like us because we had a woodstove and not a real chimney for him to slide down and land boots first in a fireplace. Then, when Mama left us, I thought it was because we really were bad. But when Aunt Belle said, "You have to have money to get toys," I thought she meant Santa had to be paid. So then I was left thinking that Santa only brought toys to rich children, because only their parents could afford to pay him. Eventually, Aunt Belle sat me and Fred Lee down and explained that toys came from the store, and Santa was only made up, to make Christmas more magical.

But even without Santa, Christmas was magical. Not only was there all the cake and pie we wanted, at any time we wanted, even at breakfast, but we also had apples, oranges, nuts, and candy for Christmas — treats we didn't have the rest of the year. Even better, Ma Pearl set those Christmas goodies in large bowls in the living room and the parlor. And we could help ourselves, without one word of chastisement.

And just where did we get all those Christmas goodies? Mrs. Robinson. But after my Thanksgiving fiasco, I decided to be grateful that day rather than resentful. I chose, for once, to be like Papa and allow contentment to unlock the door to happiness.

And happy I was. Since we had already attended church that morning, we didn't have to quote scriptures before we ate our Christmas meal. But I had one in my heart anyway: *For every creature of God is good, and nothing to be refused, if it be received with thanksgiving.*

Every creature — colored or white — is good. I knew from the lessons Reverend Jenkins had taught us that the scripture was talking about animals, and the eating of clean and unclean meats. But we, too, were creatures of God — every one of us. And he created all of us equally, just like that constitution said.

Sure, Shorty might have taunted Miss Hill that day in class saying colored folks didn't have those inalienable rights that our history text talked about, but that didn't mean we were any less than white people, or any other people. I had seen for myself what colored people were capable of doing— colored people who had once been slaves. And if colored men who had been born under the oppression of slavery could rise up and recognize their potential, then surely I, Rosa Lee Carter, though born under dire circumstances, could rise up from my situation and accomplish great things.

I didn't need Mama. I didn't need to keep pining for her and wishing she would love me and Fred Lee the way she seemed to love Sugar and Lil' Man. I had Aunt Ruthie and Miss Bertha, two women who loved me and would show me the way. Miss Bertha showed me what it meant to get an education and use it to help others. And Aunt Ruthie showed me what sacrificial love meant by the way she cared for her children. She loved them enough to find the strength to walk away from Slow John. And she loved them enough to work hard at starting a business so that she could provide for them.

Papa was right about gratitude being the key to happiness. Christmas Day was so much better than Thanksgiving had been for me. I decided not to worry about whether Johnny

Lee would show up or not. Perhaps he would have to take his wife to visit her family again and not get back in time —whatever that was supposed to mean. Regardless, I would simply enjoy the people that I already had in my life and not worry about the ones that I didn't—like Mama and Johnny Lee.

As I sat with my family in our humble home, I was grateful to be alive. Grateful to have a grandfather like Papa who loved me dearly. Grateful to have a brother like Fred Lee, who was growing up faster than I thought he would. Grateful to have an aunt like Aunt Ruthie, who smiled even when she should have been crying. And like Shorty admonished me, I was most certainly grateful to have people like the Jenkinses involved in my life.

I was grateful even to have a cousin like Queen who showed me what I didn't want to be. And Ma Pearl—yes, she was very hard on me, but as Papa said, "What don't kill you just make you stronger." Sure, she wielded her black strap of terror when she thought I needed it, but if she didn't kill Mama, Aunt Clara Jean, and Queen when they brought "shame" to her house, then surely she wouldn't kill me. And just like I wouldn't allow the Jim Crow attitude of Mississippi to chase me away from a place where my heart truly felt at home, neither would I allow her to chase me away.

The coconut cake didn't get replaced with a new one. But

Aunt Ruthie stayed up late and fixed pound cake and jelly cake because those were the only two she had ingredients for. They weren't the most delicious cakes in the world, but they would do.

But the magic of Christmas didn't end with cakes that appeared overnight, or with a Santa Claus who didn't. The magic of Christmas for me that year, 1955, happened around two in the afternoon with a knock at the door.

Aunt Ruthie and I had just finished cleaning the kitchen and were settled down in the front room, watching her girls play with the dolls that Reverend Jenkins and Miss Bertha had given them (due to a tiny hint from me). The boys were with Fred Lee in the front yard, where they had drawn a bunch of lines in the dirt in order to shoot marbles.

Papa and Ma Pearl sat in the parlor and listened to some Christmas program on the radio. And Queen had already left to spend time with Aunt Clara Jean and her family for the rest of the day.

When the knock came, Aunt Ruthie stiffened as she always did, still fearing that any day Slow John would show up and try to stake his claim on her again. Even though fear shone in her eyes, she had promised me that she would not return to him, regardless of how much he begged and promised to change.

Since Papa was in the parlor, and since it was daytime, I answered the door.

When I did, I nearly fainted.

The man standing before me was tall, as black as midnight without a moon, and a reflection of what I saw each time I peered into Ma Pearl's faded dresser mirror.

He was my daddy — Johnny Lee Banks.

Chapter Thirty-Three

SUNDAY, DECEMBER 25

My head spun like a whirlwind.

I stumbled backwards.

Johnny Lee stepped inside the door just in time. He caught me before I fell.

The world went black for a minute. When it brightened again, I was lying on the couch with my head resting on Aunt Ruthie's lap.

Papa and Ma Pearl had entered the front room, and Johnny Lee now sat in a chair. Two little girls stood next to the chair. They were not Mary Lee and Alice, Aunt Ruthie's girls. They were my sisters—Willow Mae and Betty Jean. Two little chocolate girls who looked a lot like me. Or, in the words of Joe Ann when she mentioned me to her mama, two *cute* little girls. They both wore their hair in two braids like I used to wear. And their cheeks were slightly chubby, like mine used to be, before I grew tall and skinny.

Ma Pearl barely let me raise my head before she began her chastisement. She stood over me, her arms folded over her chest, and barked, "Gal, what in the devil is wrong wit'choo?"

I shook my head and spoke weakly. "I fainted."

With a huff, she pointed at Johnny Lee. "You tell this nigga he could come to my house?"

"Mama!" Aunt Ruthie yelled.

I was shocked at Aunt Ruthie's boldness.

When Ma Pearl glared at her, Papa sternly said, "Go on back to the parlor, Pearl."

She did, but not before she scoffed at Johnny Lee and his daughters. All three of us.

"Ruthie Mae," Papa said gently. "Let's go to the kitchen and fix some coffee. This young man look like he could use a cup."

Johnny Lee nodded and said, "Much obliged, sir."

Aunt Ruthie and her girls followed Papa to the kitchen. And there I was, left in the front room with my daddy, whom I had never met, and my two little sisters, one who cuddled a little white baby doll in her arms.

The four of us sat in that front room for what felt like an eternity. Plus a day.

Finally, Johnny Lee cleared his throat and spoke. "Forgot y'all wadn't babies no mo'," he said. "I brung y'all some presents. But look like you too big for 'em now." He nudged the shorter of the two girls, whom I assumed was Betty Jean, since Shorty had said she was seven, and Willow, nine.

Betty Jean stepped forward and extended her little white baby doll toward me. "He'ah," she said. "Dis for you."

My forehead creased.

Johnny Lee chuckled at my puzzled expression. "I'on know what I was thanking. I forgot how long it been. Forgot y'all kept up with time jest like I did."

"You brought me a baby doll?"

The little girl—with two missing front teeth—grinned at me and said, "I got one jest lack it."

I took the doll and quietly said, "Thank you. I always wanted a baby doll."

Johnny Lee chuckled again and said, "I brung yo' brother a truck. You shoulda see'd his face when I give it to him."

I smiled a little as I imagined Fred Lee outside playing in the dirt with a toy truck. Like me, he had never actually expressed what toy he wished he would get for Christmas. We both knew it was pointless. But I bet a truck was probably on his mind, just like a doll had always been on mine.

I could have been angry. I could have yelled at Johnny Lee and asked him where he'd been all those years. Why did he allow Ma Pearl to keep him from visiting us? Why did I have to send a message by a cousin that I barely knew just to get him to finally come by on a holiday? Didn't he care about more than just whether Fred Lee looked like him? Didn't he care whether *I* looked like him, too? Didn't he care whether we were healthy? Or even happy?

But Papa's voice rang through my head. *Gratitude is the key to happiness, daughter. Not people.* So instead of frowning, I smiled at my daddy and thanked him again for the gifts, both mine and Fred Lee's.

Betty Jean stood there, staring at me, studying me as if I were a textbook. After a few seconds she turned to Johnny Lee and said, "She our susta f'real?"

With a wide grin, Johnny Lee said, "She sho' is. She yo' big susta."

"And her name is Rose," Willow offered, smiling too.

Betty Jean turned and stared at me a bit longer. Then she turned to Johnny Lee and asked, "She comin' to stay with us?"

Johnny Lee beckoned her to him. He shook his head and said, "Nah. Yo' susta ain't comin' with us. We jest came to see her and yo' brother." He glanced at me and, with a smile, added, "For Christmas."

Betty Jean stared at me again. Her gaze strolled from the top of my head, down my body, all the way to the tips of my socked feet. "How come she cain't come?" she asked Johnny Lee. "She ain't too big. She can sleep in my bed."

"She live here," Johnny Lee answered. "With her granmama and her papa."

Betty Jean stared curiously at Johnny Lee. "Ain't you her papa?"

With her question, I felt a bit of anger bubbling up.

Be grateful, I told myself. *When my father and my mother forsake me, then the Lord will take me up.*

I extended my hand toward Betty Jean. She came to me. I wrapped my arm around her and hugged her to my side. "Yes, I'm your big sister," I told her. I nodded toward Johnny Lee. "That's my daddy. But I live here with my grandparents because they have been my mama and daddy since I was a baby. They take care of me just like your mama and daddy take care of you."

"Can we come see her some mo'?" she asked Johnny Lee.

"We'a try," he answered.

Obviously, Ma Pearl, who could hear everything we said from the parlor, felt differently.

She stormed into the front room. "You won't be comin' nowhere, Johnny Lee Banks. 'Cause I didn't invite you here."

My two little sisters jumped. Betty Jean scurried back to Johnny Lee's side.

Ma Pearl glared at him. "You and Anna Mae ain't done nothin' but hurt these chi'ren all they lives. Y'all don't thank 'bout nobody but yo'selves." She stared down her nose at Johnny Lee, Willow Mae, and Betty Jean. "Look at ya. You jest lack Anna Mae. Run off and left this gal and that boy and started new. Jest left them for somebody else to raise like they cows and not chi'rens."

Johnny Lee held up his hands. "Ma'am, I woulda been by to see my chi'ren long time ago, but you wouldn't 'low me to. You said you'd shoot me if I ever set foot on this place. My nephew told me that the girl been astin' to see me, so I took my chances and come." He shook his head. "But I won't come no mo' if that what you want."

Ma Pearl's nostrils flared. "You dirn right it's what I want. And I want you to leave right now. And don't let yo' foots cross my do'step ever again."

Just as Johnny Lee stood to leave, Papa entered the front room. He gingerly balanced a cup of coffee atop a saucer. "Pearl?" he asked. "What's goin' on?"

"I'm showin' this fool to the do'," Ma Pearl said, pointing at Johnny Lee.

Papa sighed. "Sit down, son," he told Johnny Lee.

After Johnny Lee sat, Papa handed him the coffee. The cup rattled against the saucer as he held it.

Papa turned to Ma Pearl and said, "You ain't go'n ruin these chi'ren's time with their daddy. They done waited long enough. Now git on back to the parlor and see what that radio of yours is rattlin' about."

"Humph," Ma Pearl said with a grunt. Yet she turned and left the room.

Papa turned to me. "You enjoy this time with yo' daddy, Rose. It's precious." To Johnny Lee he said, "Come see these chi'ren anytime you want."

After he left for the kitchen, I said to Johnny Lee, "When you see Shorty, tell him I said thank you."

"I'on know when I'a see Shawty again," said Johnny Lee. "When peoples leave Miss'sippi, they ack like they'on never wanna come back."

My forehead creased in confusion. "Leave?" I asked. "Who? Shorty?"

"Yeah. Him and Papa Ray 'n'em left last night. He made sho' he stopped by first to remind me to come see you today though." He smiled and added, "But I wadn't go'n forgit."

"Shorty left?"

"For California. Charlotte came got 'em."

"His mama?"

Johnny Lee shook his head. "Nah. His aunt. Alberta his mama. Charlotte is Ray and Vee's baby girl."

"Shorty's gone to California?"

Johnny Lee nodded. "Charlotte came got him 'cause she didn't want them NAACP peoples to git holt o' him and try to make him talk at that trial o' that white man in Glendora. They started astin' 'round Glendora that next week, lookin' for folks who see'd what happened. Ray 'n'em made Shawty stay in hidin'. Couldn't even go t' school."

"That's why he stopped coming to school?" I asked.

"Um-hmm," Johnny Lee said. "They say that boy Willie Reed had a nervous breakdown after he talked 'gainst them two white mens that kil't Emmett Till. Ray 'n'em didn't want that to happen to Shawty. But Shawty wouldn't leave without him and Vee. So all of 'em left last night."

Johnny Lee sighed deeply and said, "Shawty near 'bout had a breakdown hisself after seein' that man git gunned down lack he did. He was so to'e up that he wouldn't eat."

"Shorty's gone to California?" I asked again.

"Um-hmm," Johnny Lee said.

"I can't believe it," I said. "Just like Dr. Howard in Mound Bayou." This time I spoke so quietly that I barely heard my own voice.

"What's that?" asked Johnny Lee.

"Dr. Howard in Mound Bayou. Folks say he sold all his land and left for California."

Johnny Lee shook his head. "I heard it was Chicago."

"You know about him?"

"I heard o' him. Peoples been talkin' 'bout him. Talkin' 'bout how disappointed they is in him. I ain't never put too much trust in no man myself." He pointed toward the ceiling. "Gotta put yo' trust in God." He patted his chest and said, "Gotta find yo' own strength from him and from yo' own heart."

Silence filled our space for a moment until Willow Mae asked if she could go outside and play.

Johnny Lee smiled and said, "She lack to play with trucks mo' than her brother."

With a smile in return, I said, "I was like that. I liked to play with slingshots. Do you like to climb trees, too?" I asked Willow Mae.

Grinning widely, she nodded.

"Both o' y'all go on outside," Johnny Lee said. "I'm go'n stay here and visit with Rose for a minute."

"Rosa," I said when Willow Mae and Betty Jean went outside. "My name is Rosa."

"You changed yo' name?"

I shook my head. "No. That's what Mama named me. But most folks call me Rose."

"Which one you lack best?"

"Call me Rosa," I said.

Johnny Lee visited with me until his coffee cup was

empty. We talked about everything from why he couldn't marry Mama to what my plans were for the future. Finishing high school, going to college, and taking care of my family is what I told him.

"I'm go'n talk to yo' brother for a minute, then I needs to git on back to the house," he said. "Gotta take my wife over to Kilmichael to visit her fam'ly. Thought I'd come on over here and see y'all first though."

"Shorty told me about Thanksgiving," I offered.

"I sho' felt bad 'bout that," Johnny Lee said. "Hated that I couldn't git over here 'fo the sun set. Didn't wanna upset yo' granmama mo' than she already woulda been," he said, nodding toward the parlor. He scanned the front room. "Y'all got a telephone?"

"No, sir," I said.

He shrugged. "I was go'n say you could call me when you need me, since Shawty ain't here no mo'."

"If I need you," I said, "I'll find a way to get a message to you." I wasn't too sure how that would happen, but when the time came, I was sure God would make a way.

"Don't worry. I'a come by to see y'all from time to time. I ain't go'n let nobody keep me away no mo'."

When he stood to leave, he smiled at me and said, "I'a see you again soon, Rosa."

My chest tightened. I wanted to leap up, grab my daddy by the arm, and say, "Don't leave," because I was afraid he would never come back. But the look on his face told me that he would. It wasn't a look of guilt as Mama had had that day she said goodbye to me and Fred Lee. It was a look of sincere remorse for having done wrong. A look that said, "I want to make things right."

So instead of leaping up and grabbing him by the arm, I stood and extended my hand toward him for a shake. "Thank you for coming by and for bringing us presents," I said.

Johnny Lee ignored my hand and hugged me. His hug felt awkward, but I welcomed it just the same. And when it was time for him to leave, I didn't collapse in a chair by the window and stare out, longing to join him and his family, like I had done that day back in July when Mama left. Instead, I walked out to his car with him and hugged my two little sisters.

I didn't say "Goodbye," because Papa always said that goodbye sounded too much like forever. So I waved and said, "See you again soon."

Smiling, Johnny Lee waved back and said, "You sho' will."

Life that year had been full of disappointments, tragedies, and goodbyes: my mama left, my aunt went back north, and innocent people like Emmett Till were killed. It was almost too much to bear. But there were little surprises and happy moments, too, like the unexpected visit from my daddy. Little pricks of light against the darkness. Whatever lay in store for me in the coming year, I knew that I could bear it, as long as I kept on looking for bits of hope, bits of light.

Author's Note

HELLO, WONDERFUL READER!

By now you should know that my name is Linda Williams Jackson and that I am the author of *Midnight Without a Moon* and *A Sky Full of Stars*. Like my main character, Rose, who later becomes Rosa, I was born and raised mostly on cotton plantations in the Mississippi Delta. But unlike Rose, who fictitiously lived in one place all of her life, I lived on various cotton farms during my childhood. We even lived in one house that sat right in the middle of a cotton field just like Rose's house in *Midnight Without a Moon*. And yes, we lived in what was once a sharecropper's shack. We did have electricity, however, but we did not have indoor plumbing—no indoor bathroom and no sink in the kitchen. The house also lacked common modern-day amenities such as light switches, closets, and doorknobs. Yes, doorknobs! Imagine that! Nor did we have locks on the doors that led to the outside. Our doors were secured with a small piece of wood called a latch.

According to my oldest sister, I was born on a farm called Alfred Wells's Place. (The farms, as I recall, were named for the person who owned or managed the land.) And according to my own *foggy* memory, my family lived on four different cotton farms or "places" during my early years. In January 1978, when I was eleven and a half years old, in the middle of a rare Mississippi snowstorm, we moved to town and never again lived on a cotton farm. Mickey Dattel's Place was the last farm on which we lived. Yet, even after we moved, I spent the next three years wishing I could go back to country living. I was an extremely shy child, so I hated living in town where everyone could see me and know what was happening in my day-to-day life. During the summer of 1978 — our first summer living in town — I didn't leave the house *at all* for a whole month.

Now, one would think that living in a sharecropper's shack on an old cotton plantation would be the worst fate a child of the 1970s could have. But even though times were hard (really hard), those were some of the best years of my life. They were my formative years, my coming-of-age years. And it was those years, or the essence of them, that I wanted to capture and bring back to life in *Midnight Without a Moon* and *A Sky Full of Stars*.

Although my life was very different from Rose's, I am indeed the granddaughter of a sharecropper. Like Rose, I called my grandfather Papa. Papa's character in *Midnight Without a Moon* is based loosely on stories I heard about my own grandfather, Thad Scott. Rose's situation—being left behind in the South to be raised by her grandparents—comes from the real-life plight of many children growing up during the time African Americans were migrating from the South to the North. But Rose's character is purely fictional, with a few sprinkles of my own life tossed in.

I have always wanted to write a story about my family's life in the Mississippi Delta, but I didn't know what I wanted to write about specifically. I didn't know how to narrow the story down to a single plot.

Then one night while watching the news with my mother, we heard a reference to the Emmett Till murder. My mother, who at this time had begun to slightly slip into dementia, made the comment, "I sure believe Mr. So-and-So had something to do with killing that boy." I can't recall the exact name she used, but all of sudden, her words struck me. My mother had never spoken about Emmett Till before, so I had no clue she knew anything about his murder. She would have been twenty-seven years old at that time, but like it was for so many people, the tragedy must have been so shocking to her that she had refused to even mention it until she was in her late seventies. It was as if the dementia —the forgetting of things present—had brought back ghosts from the past.

Still wanting to write a book that somehow weaved in family stories, I began to wonder what life must have been like for my family in 1955. Also, as a writer, I wanted to write about the Emmett Till story because most of the books about it had been written by people who were not from Mississippi. As a Delta native, I wanted to provide readers a close look at that tragic, pivotal time in our nation's history.

The great novelist Toni Morrison is attributed with saying, "If there's a book that you want to read, and it hasn't been written yet, then you must write it." *Midnight Without a Moon* and *A Sky Full of Stars* are the books that I wanted to read, and since they had not been written, I wrote them myself.

Who would've thought those hard times growing up in the Mississippi Delta would one day help me fill the pages of two books? I hope you enjoyed reading them as much as I enjoyed writing them.

With all my love,
Linda Williams Jackson

Acknowledgments

THANK YOU!

Elizabeth Bewley and Nicole Sclama. (My Exceptional Editors!)

Victoria Marini. (My Awesome Agent!)

Genetta Adair and Caroline Flory. (My Wonderful Writer Friends!)

All the fabulous folks at Houghton Mifflin Harcourt Books for Young Readers who made this book possible.

And God, through whom all things are possible!!!